T0193247

The Melting Pot: 1919-1939

The Melting Pot: 1919-1939

Jean Romano

THE MELTING POT: 1919-1939

iUniverse books may be ordered through booksellers or by contacting:

iUniverse
1663 Liberty Drive
Bloomington, IN 47403
www.iuniverse.com
1-800-Authors (1-800-288-4677)

ISBN: 978-1-5320-8825-4 (sc)
ISBN: 978-1-5320-8826-1 (e)

Library of Congress Control Number: 2019918290

Print information available on the last page.

iUniverse rev. date: 11/08/2019

Preface

This story begins exactly one hundred years before the time it is written. The problems remain as urgent now as then. They have altered to meet the times but essentially Americans still seek to define what our country is at its core.

Immigration has always been at the forefront of American thought. Immigrants were sought at times, limited by quotas, checked for skills, brought as slaves, and banned by race or religion. Many argue that the tremendous advantage of America is the diversity of perspectives and abilities gathered under one flag. One person's approach to a problem is as likely to fail or succeed as another but we have the advantage of many options. With different ways of dissecting an issue there is hope for a solution.

Gender issues come and go as well. The points of view on any concern are affected by gender as well as ethnicity. Separation of the two offers an incomplete answer to any question. All women do not think alike nor do all men. The melting pot that is America includes the power of all influences regardless of gender, race, or ethnicity. After World War I, it was clear that the energy and skill of women extended far from the kitchen. The effect of women seeking an opportunity to lead is clearer in the 21st century and unlikely to fade.

Organizations founded on hate towards "the other" were strong one hundred years ago and they flourish in 2019 as well. The KKK in the 1920's called on its members to fight against Blacks, Catholics, and Jews. During World War I, German Americans were closely watched and some were placed in internment camps. It was the correct decision for some but the effects covered all hyphenated Americans. Is hate better on an individual basis? Or do we need armed militias and independent avengers to ensure a pure, and perhaps, white majority. The power of the Nazi party in Germany before the Second World War should be a warning against the use of hate to achieve national goals.

Add to these issues the question of income inequality. What human needs are the responsibilities of the society? Can a country be strong without empowering all of its citizens or without educating all its citizens for the future? How much talent is lost through segregation for any reason?

Majority rule is an inspirational and democratic term. Majorities are often wrong in their choices and so our government makes corrections through constitutional means. Elections are only one way of setting policy and national goals.

Much of this moment could be dated at an earlier time. Those that do not read history are destined to repeat it.

Authors' Note

The characters in the story are fictitious but the historical settings are not. The tale began with immigrants from Germany in the late 19th century in a book called *Over the Rhine*. This story begins with the close of World War I. Country of origin is as important as the time in history. Immigrants at one stage of a historical era are very different than those living in another and some are in favor at one point in history but not the next. Lives are influenced by what is taking place where immigrants came from and what is happening where they are settling to begin anew.

The characters in the story are influenced by those variables that are still very real in America. "What is your country of origin?" is still a question asked of those who sound different, look different, or act differently than their neighbors or the questioner. "Send Them Back" is a chant heard at recent political rallies.

Elise Holtz Freimarck did not rest often or easily. She accomplished much by keeping on schedule, separating family, community, and world affairs into tidy compartments in her mind. In some cases, this was necessary to keep peace in the family, in others it meant keeping the greater peace for all. Elise learned her place in this process.

Both before and after her marriage to Frank Freimarck, Elise was part of two entities: Cincinnati proper and the close packed community of German immigrants. In childhood, Elise learned in both German and English. Her own interest resulted in a strong background in the culture of Germany. Her mother's ambitions ensured she attended the best school that could "finish" a young woman's education and prepare her for entrance to upper class society. Elise's lack of skill in embroidery and other feminine endeavors was a trial to her mother. Her beauty made up for other disabilities, but not to Elise.

"After all," her mother sighed to herself alone, "the Lorelei just had to sit on a rock and sing."

Elise's need to connect with her German heritage kept her in contact with the Over the Rhine district of the city. At the beginning of World War I, while America remained neutral, Elise tried to connect families of recent immigrants with their relatives in Germany. She developed an extensive listing of contacts in local government offices in Germany and had managed to bring some news to Cincinnati residents before the threat of being labeled a sympathizer or worse stopped her effort. But after the armistice, the lists formed the base for work towards reuniting families.

Elise and her mother, a nurse, volunteered to assist the Red Cross in humanitarian relief efforts in Germany after the November 1918 Armistice. For over two months, she had helped the Red Cross locate families separated by the war. She found the parents of children in hospitals and helped the wounded return home. The journey was designed, in part, to find her brother, Herman, missing in action. She did find him, a joyful end to a sad premonition that she had caused his death.

In a short time, Elise Holtz had lived many lives: a beautiful golden girl who ruled her brothers in the nursery, a bullied girl in finishing school, a recognized beauty and competitor who won the city's most eligible bachelor, an inept bride and social leader, a woman in love with a stranger, a star visitor in Germany, a woman in love for the first time with her husband. And then the return to Germany to assist the ruined country after WWI ended. Through these changes Elise developed confidence in her own abilities and a deep love for her home and family. The regret she held for her problems as a girl served to impel her towards justice for all. She lost only one attribute: her waist-long blonde hair was left on the floor of a camp hospital in Germany.

By 1919, Elise was back home in Cincinnati. As the years flew past, Elise's family was composed of parents who became citizens, their American born children, and their children's children who were second generation Americans. World War I brought many changes: the Holtz grandchildren would be educated far differently than their parents.

We ask now what new arrivals bring with them. That is also what we asked in years past. When we wanted laborers, Africans were brought as slaves and they helped the South become an economic power through the production of cotton. Chinese came to build our railroads, Irish, Italians and Poles worked in construction and in factories. What do we want of immigrants now? That is not quite clear but it has begun to be put into words by our government.

Part One

The End Of World War I

Chapter 1

Looking Ahead

Early one morning, Elise sat in a chair, her long golden hair lit by the sunlight from an east-facing window. The sitting room was part of the master bedroom she and her husband, Frank, shared. It faced the front of the house giving an opportunity to see who was arriving before descending the stairs. Two chairs, separated by a round table, faced a fireplace. Her cat, Olga, was comfortably settled but still watchful, every nerve ending poised to detect sudden movements. The cat was part of the family for Elise if not for Frank.

"Puss is thinking 'life is good at the moment but to escape possible danger a one must stay alert'. How like a cat," Elise said to Frank, "And we could all take a lesson from her. I have that feeling of something around the corner, waiting to jump out and eat me alive."

"Why do you sense danger, my dear, on this lovely sunny day?" Frank was smiling while preparing to explain the news of his departure. He thought of Puss as "Katze Drei" and had no particular interest in its message.

"I know you have news, Frank, why don't you tell me

about it now while I am sitting still and writing the day's schedule? The women are meeting tomorrow. I will be going to the Community Center at 10:00. Our agenda is set – that is, the Organizing Committee has set an agenda, but it may not be easy to get the votes we need to carry it out."

"Can you give me an idea of what it is? My news will wait. And, you said danger and now you have all of my attention. I confess you did not when I came in the door! It was just so good to see you here, at home, with Puss on your lap. I missed you, worried about you, and spent much time waiting for a letter announcing that you and Herman would soon be here. I can also add that the children were in need of their mother. That was a dangerous situation for sure!" Frank sat down and reached out to touch her hand. That was the signal for Puss to leap off her comfy lap and flee.

Elise looked at Frank and realized how much she had missed home. She knew their marriage began in truth a few years after the ceremony itself and she was just becoming comfortable with Frank as a husband.

And Elise began to explain her current schedule. She and Louisa, her brother Willie's wife, were serious about the formation of a strong women's organization, including the German community, bringing them the ability to vote and allowing their voices to be heard. Columbus led the way but Cincinnati was not far behind. By expanding the network, Elise felt it was possible that many former immigrant wives would be on the voting lists in the next election. They came with their husbands or as single women. Their influence was felt only at home. Soon they would be able to help guide their new country in the values and ideals that brought them so far. Elise was also concerned for the education of women. She still felt the disparity placed on her own.

Elise gave Frank a complete schedule for the next month's activities. She and Louisa were planning for the future. The Organization of Women Voters would provide a base for confirming that all were citizens and it would also ensure that all citizens would have a vote. Even women. With all respect, Elise and others could not believe the 14th amendment allowed former slaves to vote, that is, if they were men, but that women could not. The word "male" was prominent in the amendment. Women had been important in the nursery, church and kitchen, but not in the political life of their new country. This had to change. The meeting planned would set a schedule of rallies, meetings, informational tracts in English and German, and contacts for sources of help.

Her explanations were clear and well received. Frank listened patiently and then gave some ideas on the how to go about the process. He knew Elise had the skills to accomplish all the goals she described. The mood was changing and it appeared that President Wilson would back a new amendment for Women's Suffrage. The time was now, the war had ended and the country was ready to make some changes. It was so calm a discussion that Puss re-entered the room and composed herself on Elise's lap.

How different life had been a few years past. Elise began her married life under the rigid guidance of Frank's mother and only slightly less oversight by her own. All other aspects of her activities, dress, and social duties were under the scrutiny of her sisters-in-law, and, eventually the nanny. It is unfortunate that war is sometimes the catalyst for the advancement of women. This last thought was not expressed to many.

Elise had not yet taken time to sort through the many events that were behind her activities. Louisa was one of her few school friends, not an immigrant family but a young woman whose mother had been divorced. No one would look beyond the action to place blame as it was assumed a woman divorced must have done something truly bad. At their school, Elise and Louisa found comfort in each other that lasted long past graduation. They made a natural team for the project ahead.

Frank nodded his approval of Elise's plans. Puss was purring on her lap. Suddenly, clouds hid the sun. The door burst open and was stopped only by the wall next to it. Puss departed and Eva, Frank's mother stepped into the room. Elise instinctively tried to follow the cat but was stopped by a rush of confidence in her power to cope.

"How wonderful to see you, mother!" Elise said this with an inviting smile. The smile would enrage her mother-in-law and that was the objective.

Chapter 2

Eva in Control

Eva Freimarck was dressed fashionably. The weight she carried added emphasis to her confident stride. At the moment, she was sure of her mission. Elise must be stopped and quickly. She would cause damage to her husband's reputation, her children's development, her mother's health and the family business Frank managed. All of these concerns were of greater importance than giving women the vote and it was time for Elise to feel the iron will of her husband's mother. She did not count the damage to herself but it was obvious: she was losing control of the family. She stepped into the room knowing only a dedicated mother could have the nerve to do this, and gathered her thoughts.

"And after I spent years raising her children!" Eva was quickly working into a rage. No matter that she had insisted on bringing up the children of her beloved Frank. Not even Elise's mother had put any objections in the way of her complete control. The nanny was carefully vetted, hired and paid for by Eva, and she reported to Eva alone. If Elise ventured a question, Nanny May quickly remembered an immediate action she was pledged to fulfill. And this was done on specific orders from Eva. As these thoughts flashed through her mind, Eva smiled again.

"Perhaps we should move to the breakfast room where we can all sit?" Elise made it clear that the room they were in did not have space for a mother-in-law

Earlier, when she had carefully engineered Elise's solitary trip to Germany, Eva carefully placed her own emissary in the position of Elise's maid. Elise's former maid had tried but failed to give Elise the gravitas Eva sought for her. And so Elise was awarded a new companion more appropriate in background and responsible to her employer Eva.

Elise and Sonia became as close as two women can. She was devastated when Sonia decided to marry and stay in Germany. Eva never knew that Sonja's allegiance had changed during the time abroad. In Eva's defense, Elise had never protested any plan of action suggested by her mother-in-law. Elise tried to overcome this feeling of ceding power without a fight when she was a bride. Those days were long gone.

Frank was watching her, saw the smile, and responded with his own smile and cautionary-raised eyebrows. As they walked down stairs to the breakfast room Eva's pulse rate dropped and she carefully sat down on a cushioned chair. The interval between arrival and relocation took minutes but put the three on neutral ground. "One should never have to discuss things with a mother-in-law in the bedroom." Elise had made this a rule.

Eva Batzberg Freimarck was the daughter of Julius Batzberg, a journalist of Jewish descent who decided to come to America with his wife, Helga, in 1863. He was connected with News sources and arrived with a job in hand. His wife had been part of the decision he made to convert to Christianity but surprisingly, she became a leading supporter of the Alliance Israelite in Berlin and a vocal critic of Russia's treatment of the Jewish community in that country. These liberal roots translated well to America and Julius reported on the Civil War for newspapers in Europe and then, in his new home. Eva enjoyed the family, guiding each one into a proper life-style. Her liberal views did not carry over to the wife of her beloved son Frank.

Eva was brought up to respect the values of her parents and her country of birth, America. Her one blind spot was her son Frank. He was followed by two sisters, Augusta and Gertrud, whose obedience to Eva was unequivocal.

Frank had been set on a path designed to give him the best education possible, an ability to study and learn in both German and English, and the freedom to develop his own opinions of the world around him. In addition, he was a good athlete, drawing more supporters into his orbit. Eva's life-long goals were wrapped around Frank and this eventually included the development of his wife and bringing up of their children.

Elise was a choice made as much by Eva as her son. Elise had beauty, physical stamina, an education, German roots, and, most important, she was under the thumb of her mother in all things. When Eva assessed the situation, she knew that after her transfer from the Holtz family to the Freimarck camp, she would be able to manage Elise through her metamorphosis as the perfect wife for her son. And when they came, the children would also be molded into replicas of their father. Bless him. Bless them all. The transfer had gone extremely well. Eva approved Elise initial trip to Germany and then her tour of duty after World War I ended. She rejoiced when Elise found her brother Herman and she was among the first to welcome him home. Clearly, Elise owed her a lot; she just had to recognize it.

Since returning home with Herman, Elise had slowly and surely taken hold of the reins. The children had a new nanny and Elise headed her own household. In addition, she had become active in the community once again. Her early efforts to create a network for German immigrants and their families in the old country had been stopped when war began. It was clear, even to Elise, that such out reach could be misunderstood. And now she was using that network to organize and affect the vote for immigrant women. Unfortunately, despite all the liberal beliefs in her heart, Eva still felt church, kitchen, and children were the purview of wives. True, the symphony, art, opera and nature could add to the personal attributes of a wife. But the vote? Politics? Demonstrations? Decidedly not.

Frank was more curious than worried about this confrontation. It had to come. It had been coming. He knew who would win. And now that he was sure that his wife could resolve this issue without him, he stood and spoke. "Mama, Elise is organized enough to complete all her traditional duties and to take on some of the issues we both feel are of great importance. Yes, I do believe that women should vote. It may save us all from making the same mistakes we have made in the past. Mother, let us count the blessings of this family without looking backwards," Frank began his new strategy with a smile. "Elise so appreciates your time with our children, most especially during the time she was away. She needs to reacquaint herself with them and to build on what you accomplished. They are on the way to being well educated, socially adept, and emotionally secure. And Elise will still ask your guidance in matters of importance. For now, they live with us and hold their love for you deep in their hearts."

Eva sighed and relinquished her grandchildren. She was not sure how deep in their hearts she resided, at least with Frank and Elise's offspring. Her two daughters still needed her full attention, and it is true, she wasn't as young as before the war. Eva was not really upset by the change she could see it coming.

"Perhaps you are right, Frank. I have some other interests that have been on hold and I will now begin to look outside the family. And, Elise, there are things I would like to discuss with you. Let us set a time, each week, to talk about the future."

Elise lost her smile, but for just a moment. "Of course, Mama! It will be a pleasure!"

Eva had not known Frank's thoughts on this matter and she realized she should have touched base with him before this visit. In fact, Eva's opposition to the cause of women's suffrage was the reason for this encounter; she was blind-sided by the switch to the grandchildren. Her mind skipped back a few steps and recovered an argument carefully designed before she left home. But before she could advance the need for Elise to return to tradition, Frank spoke again.

"I have some very big news for you ladies, and for the family. I will be away from home for some time, and then back and forth to carry out my new responsibilities. Your help will ensure my success. Please consider this change in our lives as important enough to build a new kind of tradition. Tonight we will all be together and I will tell you my assignment."

This was not the way Frank intended to pass on his news, but it might be better to share it with the entire family circle at one meeting. He would talk to Elise as soon as his mother had gathered her belongings and left to plan the night ahead.

And feeling the need to move, Eva kissed Elise on both cheeks, smiled at Frank, straightened her scarf and spine and left the room.

"Well done, Frank!" Elise laughed at the speed of resolution. She was calmly prepared for Eva but appreciative of the reprieve. "I knew you would approve of our work with the vote. Bettie Wilson has become a celebrity in Cincinnati and she is retiring soon. I want to work with her before she is gone. And, of course, our President has at last come before Congress to endorse votes for women. No longer a dangerous issue. Am I right?"

"As always." He was surprised to hear himself say this but it was true. He trusted Elise to get it right. As he thought back he recalled his first surprise on visiting Germany when Elise was there as a guest of his mother's family. Not only was she happy, glowing, and surrounded by gentlemen, it was her conversation in German that caused him to reassess his wife. He didn't realize her German was better than his and the content she was sharing matched his own knowledge of what was happening at home and abroad. He completed his business in somewhat of a daze, accepting the congratulations of family and friends on his choice of a wife. He longed for the privacy of their ship's cabin on the long voyage home. Max was born nine months later.

Frank's attention came back to the present. There were some drawbacks to having an intelligent and attractive wife but this was not the time to dwell on them.

Chapter 3

Frank

Frank Freimarck was a handsome man who showed some of the results of good living, but with grace. Childhood was a time of intense physical activity and he looked Olympian to some. There were no curls but his hair was a shade of yellow that contrasted with his dark brown eyes and ruddy skin. If Frank did not attract attention when he entered a room he considered leaving and entering again with louder trumpets playing. He enjoyed being the center of attention.

His former love of soccer continued but only as a spectator. Baseball caught his attention late in life. He was now a Reds fan primarily and deeply immersed in the season ahead. In truth, his purchase of season box seats was for business purposes. The box was always full of clients, businessmen, and their wives or friends. Elise did not see the point of baseball and Frank was happy with her decision to skip the season.

The family business was successful because of Frank's ability to establish ties in Germany and several other European countries that traded with the U.S. Before the war he made frequent trips to Germany and he was well acquainted with the state of research, manufacturing and technical innovation happening there. After WWI began, America exported goods and materials to the Allies and the Germans under the laws of neutrality until America joined the Allied effort to defeat Germany in 1917.

Frank reflected on his own stance. "I believed in American democracy, in its support of our allies and their cause. It was clear for some time that Germany was preparing for war. My grandfather, a military man, left Germany because of the direction it took years ago. And yet in Germany I am considered a man of substance. It was just luck that I didn't get distracted."

Nevertheless, the F & B Manufacturing Company continued to export many products. American foodstuffs and even cotton were part of the ship cargos leaving for ports across the Atlantic. Frank was the main contact between many exporters and he did it as a service, making him a popular figure in the business world on both sides of the ocean. His business was with England and France after the British blockade sealed off Germany and those under its influence or occupation. Businessmen from the eastern seaboard and the mid-west were well acquainted with his connections. He was consulted by many, and after the war, by an equal number of legislators.

"How I survived the anti-German feeling during those years is a mystery to me." Frank completed his musings aloud and then concentrated on the task at hand. Elise had all his support in a venture soon to be endorsed by the President. Her intelligence still surprised him, he had thought of her as an inexperienced mother, a social misfit in Cincinnati society, a mother dominated daughter, and a less than helpful wife. Now he recognized her worth and appreciated her help. Whatever he proposed to his own mother would be accepted so there were no impediments at home.

Frank's success now seemed an omen. He was about to tell the family of his call to Washington for meetings with several Cabinet members. Recommendations had come from more than one person, and not all came from Ohio. Frank was hoping to enter the world stage as an American. As he said to himself, "I am an American now, not a German-American." And he was glad for any diversions that would ensure focus on his expertise in business.

At this point, the Red Scare was considered even more of a threat to the United States than the defeated Germans. Just a few years past, anti-German sentiment would have denied any thought of a German-American, even one born in the States, to a position in government. The Espionage Act of 1917 and the Sedition Act of 1918 set the stage for severe reaction against the enemies of the country. Dissent and criticism of the government was enough to ensure jail time without a hearing. Many immigrants were arrested for no reason other than their ancestry.

The diversion of the Russian Revolution in 1917 brought fears of a government overthrow engineered by revolutionaries. Union organizers were conflated with anarchists. Fear of immigrants did not end, however, as immigrant populations grew.

Frank knew that his background had already been carefully checked. "Thank God Elise's father did complete his citizenship. I didn't think he would be allowed to apply except for the work of his wife and daughter. And, of course, his mastery of all things mechanical was helpful. That was the plus. The Irish and Italians and Asians often brought only the ability to conduct hard labor.

"Wilhelm, excuse me, William, was lucky." Frank said this to thin air but he was happy with the thought.

It did seem that America would not join the League of Nations. This was a great disappointment to President Wilson who had strong hopes for his 14 Points. The people were not in a mood to unite with the wreckage of Europe. This isolation was a problem in a world that needed cooperation to recover from the last five years of war. The U.S. would send representatives to committee meetings and a presence was necessary – one that had credibility and contacts. Frank had been noticed

The Department of Commerce and the Department of Labor, needed a few more good men. Since the Constitution for the League had been drafted at the Paris Peace Conference in January and was waiting for acceptance by the 44 member States, it was time to organize a team from America to attend future meetings of newly established committees if only as representatives.

"I am being given a trial appointment. There are no guarantees of acceptance. My reputation is high and I have skills and knowledge that are unique. Why wouldn't they want me to be in Washington?" Frank was pacing the floor and looking for flaws in his character that would deny him this chance. "I can't think of any reason they would pass me by for another."

"Now, what do I tell the family? It is not a bad time to leave. Mother is occupied with my sisters' children. Elise is over-scheduled with children and Women's' Suffrage issues, and Willie and William will somehow keep the company afloat. In fact, our orders make us solvent for the next two years. I cannot say too much as some of this is not information I can share. Which of the family might oppose this step?"

A hesitant knock on the library door stopped his thoughts.

Chapter 4

Louisa and Willie

66 **F**rank, I have heard that your mother is concerned about my activity in the Suffrage movement and my influence on Elise. Willie told me to ask you if this will be harmful to the family. Those years of being German-Americans have made him cautious and he is still worried about Herman's story. Will those opposed to your position bring this out in the open?" Louisa paused for breath. She did not want to talk to Frank about this and she most certainly did not want to be told to stop her devotion to the cause of women's rights.

And Frank obliged. "You follow your heart, Louisa. Please know I appreciate your concerns. Women's suffrage is coming, perhaps sooner than you think. I have heard that the President will soon give it his approval. And I agree. Herman's story is perhaps the biggest block to my acceptance. It is a reminder of our ancestry and another piece of information that can be used to question my loyalty and the family as well. But you have brought it up and I am grateful. I will be prepared." Frank kissed her cheek and asked to be excused. Louisa always gave him a moment of unease. Unlike almost every lady he had met over the years, she never reacted to his presence with any personal response.

Louisa looked like a person who would be dedicated to a cause. She dressed as comfortably as possible in the style of past times, wore her hair in a bun, and left off any trace of paint or powder. In truth, she never thought much about her appearance. Her attendance at meetings never evoked comments on how she was dressed. Since childhood, Louisa had felt outside the group and she no longer felt a need to follow changes in fashion, only in dedication to change in the social fabric.

Louisa's first connection to the family came through her finishing school experience with Elise. The two girls each had problems that were not easily remedied. Elise had standards based on her mother's perception of what a good German girl should be doing, basically, obeying her mother. Louisa, as the daughter of a divorcee, had a more mysterious aura. The imaginings of what her mother might have done made her interesting but the fear of becoming involved in the story made her frightening. In other words, her classmates resisted the call to become friends, just in case they might be infected.

Over the years Louisa had championed the rights of women. Her mother had done nothing to earn rejection by society except to be a wife and mother with a roving husband. And, of course, it was her fault.

Ir doesn't seem likely but Elise and Louisa had more than one common thread to join them in friendship. The same problem of an absent husband was one of Elise's issues. Frank was as excellent businessman only because of his extreme dedication to the office, or so he told her when questioned. While Emilia deferred to Frank's mother in all things, Louisa gave advice to her own parent. Elise was never asked for an opinion or a decision on a course of action. Louisa was on her own. It was harder for Louisa as an only child. Elise had the support and love of her brothers who were shocked by her metamorphosis from daredevil childhood to prim nothingness. It was a cross-cultural friendship made in the USA.

Louisa was a student at the finishing school at the same time as Elise. This bond brought them closer and after several visits to Elise's home she met all of the family. Her help with Willie after his accident was critical for them all. Louise continued her studies with Willie as her mentor and companion into their adulthood. Louisa was able to enter University with help from her father who had kept in touch and was well able to assist his daughter. She was a fast learner and although considered unfeminine, she won respect and Willie's heart. They married in a quiet wedding with only the best of their friends and family in attendance.

Willie and Louisa collaborated on papers and the research involved in Willie's graduate research role at the University of Cincinnati. They had no children as yet, freeing Louisa for a foray into the Hamilton country branch of the Women's Suffrage Association, led by Bettie Wilson. Its message gave her an outlet for the sorrow she still felt for her mother's treatment. And as the years passed during the First World War,

Louisa noted the many new tasks taken on by women with great success. She was devoted to the work done to enfranchise women and finally, she asked Elise if she might be interested in bringing the suffrage movement to the German community, still intact and still in the section of Cincinnati nearest the Ohio River and still called Over the Rhine.

The three met less than a week ago to discuss the best means of approaching the women. "They are still in the traditional mind set and that will be a problem. Perhaps we can invite the younger girls to start the process? We can show them as models to their mothers."

"If the mothers have any idea that their daughters will be more involved, knowledgeable, and active than they are we are lost. My hope is to locate those women who actually worked during the war years. They have been away from the hearth just long enough to tempt them on to greater things. And, since their standard of living improved with two wages, they may gain their husbands approval." Elise used her own experience to add this idea.

The two women were seated in the sunny breakfast room of a small apartment Louisa and Willie rented near the University. Elise had managed to have her hair bobbed and a day of shopping with her sister-in-law, Augusta, changed her into a modern woman. Dropped waist, t-strapped shoes and rolled stockings gave her a different appearance than her closest friend. No one would ever have realized they spent hours together. The subject of clothing never was discussed.

Willie was smiling and quiet as yet. Now he spoke.

"Elise, you used these same tactics in the nursery. None of us realized that your skills would be submerged for so long, you are the perfect example of a woman's place in the world in the past and the possibilities for the future. And, because I haven't told you before, I truly approve of your bobbed hair. I know you did it while serving with the Red Cross after the war but you could easily have grown it back by now. Good for you, you always hated the maintenance involved in yards of hair." He laughed and so did Elise. Her mother sighed each time Elise returned from her monthly trim.

Louisa and Elise began to respond at the same time. "We must..._" "OK, you first Louisa!" And so carefully and slowly Louisa warned them. "This may be very unpopular in the community where they live and in the city at large. Actions against some women from England to Ohio are already reported. We may be putting them in danger and they should know this from the start. The other concern I must speak to is the fact that we are still, and may always be hyphenated Americans. Experiences during the war against some with a German background were varied and they may not be fully gone. Let's take the time to look into what is happening in Cincinnati now before stepping into the battle."

What had seemed an exciting and necessary adventure took a solemn turn. "We will do this. Louisa has spoken of it to Frank. I trust his good judgment. I will speak to our father who is devoted to the local newspapers and you, Elise will find out what our mother thinks of this." Willie had set up a process and they could begin. "We will meet again in one week." Willie got up from his chair. He had not been invited to the table but he effectively closed the conversation with a charge to each participant.

Willie was two years younger than his sister, Elise. He truly had the look of the Nordic male, blonde and blue-eyed. Due to a childhood accident, he had lost a leg. His life had been limited but not his mind. He pursued his studies with vigor and was enrolled in an advanced degree program at the University. His field had been thought of as far in the future but the war had hastened its acceptance. Willie was fast becoming an expert on the effects of economic policies and the development of industry and the wealth of nations. His earnest appearance helped. Trousers covered his leg brace, and, for short distances he could walk without a limp. He still needed self -confidence to be a good lecturer but with Louisa, he was beginning to get that in line with his ambitions. "How I miss Herman! His advice was always too daring but he did give us goals to reach that were not easy but important." Willie was a team player and his idea of a "team" was growing quickly.

They were about to leave until the thought of Herman came to the front. All three sat silently for a moment. Elise had found Herman in a Canadian hospital after the war. He had been shot down while flying in France. He was badly burned, and unable to recall who or where he was. This trauma saved him for he was identified as Canadian although he had been flying with the German air force. Throughout his time in a recovery hospital in Canada, his only communication had been "I want to go home" spoken in English. Since his return to Cincinnati, he received the care and love of family but not one of them was sure he knew who they were.

No, the effort described would be left to Elise, Louise, and one male with good sense. They would meet again and then design their plans. "Look at the time!" Willie and Elise spoke at the same moment. The meeting Frank called will start in an hour! Perhaps Frank will set a tone that leads this family into new territory!"

Elise looked pale and her brother feared the stress of the coming meeting was already showing. He asked her if she would be able to get through the questions from family that he could predict.

Elise answered him in a wobbly voice. "I will do my best to support Frank. But, Willie, I do not feel myself and hope it is not an indication of taking on more than I can do."

And Willie said, "We will all support each other and Frank will set the stage for our activities. I am planning to bring Herman along just to smother him with relatives and perhaps pierce his shell!"

"If anything will do it, that is the time and place! Imagine, all of us together, in one room, listening to news from Frank!" Louise laughed at the idea, Willie looked thoughtful, and Elise decided she might faint.

Chapter 5

The Meeting

Eva had come and gone, Louisa and Willie left, reassured that all would be well, and only Elise needed Frank's full explanation. Louisa knew something was going to happen. Frank had been even more invisible than usual, pleading the stress of work. True, the business needed a steady hand but aside from retooling and rethinking its purpose, the economic problems arising were beyond Frank's expertise. His time with Willie had doubled this last month.

Elise slipped back into the room. "Is all clear? I do not want to interfere with your many visitors but perhaps you have a moment to tell me what is going to be announced in less than an hour?"

And briefly, Frank told her of a call from the Capitol and his role in devising a path forward for the country's business. He had left out a few pieces of his charge and one new concern had been added with Louisa's visit. Would Herman's story end this whole adventure? He looked at Elise but his mind was far away. Despite his childhood in Cincinnati and his graduation from Harvard, Frank still felt an outsider at times. He wanted to be accepted as the American citizen he was. Clearly his wife was an ally. With luck, her family would not be the enemy. He excused himself and went up stairs to change.

Frank had called the family meeting so that he could be sure everyone had the same story. In a family such as his, misinterpretations occurred often with the best o intentions. This time, they would all have identical information at the same time. It was not that he worried about a lack of support; it was more that his new position would be debated and cause discord. The hope was to provide a united front to anyone wondering what he was doing. It was too bad he did not have time to brief Elise separately. He heard a call from below. Frank left the bedroom, walked down a very long hallway, turned to the left and waited for Elise to appear. He looked over the bannister at the marble foyer many feet below him. He loved his home.

The long porch led to a double door. This opened into the foyer, a marble delight that was as wide as the house itself. The long staircase began at the far wall. Behind the stair was a stained glass window that gave the area a bath of many colors when the sun was shining. Turn left and you were in the living room, on the right, pocket doors opened into the dining room. A huge chandelier hung the length of the space from the second floor to mid-entry level.

The bell rang and the arrivals began to enter. The front door remained open as the family arrived by carriage, by foot, and by auto.

Jean Romano

First to arrive were Louisa and Willie. They had brought Herman with them, perhaps for good luck? Then his mother marched in, ready for battle. Although Frank's father had died, she never missed a family conference and even initiated one when she felt it time. Her two daughters and their husbands were with her to ensure the majority if a vote became in order. Of course, Herman had no say. And then Emilia and William, completing the immediate family members.

The years preceding the First World War had been lucrative for F & B Industries. Gradually the British blockade had squeezed the exports from the US so that Britain and France were the only ports able to accept delivery. And when war was declared by the US and all appearance of neutrality gone, business was still brisk and the needs of America increasing. And now, with Germany in dire shape, losing population, factories, raw materials and buying power, it was a time to rebuild on an international scale. Frank desperately wanted to show his loyalty and his skill in equal parts. His opportunity came shortly after the Armistice.

President Wilson had split one Department into two: Commerce and Labor. The workings of the new League of Nations would provide much work for both. The US did not join the League of Nations but did cooperate and send representatives to committees. The 14 points set out by Woodrow Wilson did survive in some form and they are still referred to today, but in Frank's time, they were the basis of US policy. He planned to manage them well to advance the profits of his own company, using William

Holtz's technical knowledge, Willie's financial acumen, and the Batzberg financial backing.

The group milled about. The room was large and it accommodated at least three groupings of chairs and sofas. Eva directed her charges to one area and had some furniture moved to give them room and a tactical position. The others filled in wherever they found seating. Emilia stayed close to Herman but William and Willie chose to sit apart from the rest. It seemed that everyone was enjoying a social event and Frank finally tapped on his chair back to bring some kind of order. All were silent and expectant except for Eva who had some final words for her daughters. Frank tapped again. It was not the silence of the tomb but it would do.

Frank outlined the current politics in Washington and explained the role he would play. It would take him away from Cincinnati for a period of time but it would give him a reputation that would advance their fortunes and those were tied to the growth of the national economy. It had to be a winning strategy. Frank also brought up the issue all in the room were aware of: the attitude towards German-Americans at the moment.

Neither brother-in-law was of German descent. Augusta married Roger Taft and her sister Gertrude wed John Alden. Both families were long-term residents of Ohio, arriving earlier in the 19th century than the Batzbergs, the Freimarcks or the Holtz families. The two brothers-in-law chose their wives more for their new money than their ties to old society. Frank counted on their involvement in F & B but worried about the concessions that could be exacted for their inclusion in the company. William Holtz wanted firm control over the methods and materials of production. Frank wanted control over exports, trade deals and imports. Eva wanted control over the distribution of profits. It surely could be worked out.

When William rose to explain the shift from armaments to peacetime products, Herman grew agitated. "No, no, no," he stammered but just hearing him speak electrified the group. Herman was hearing what was said and he had joined the discussion. It was considered a miracle by them all.

Willie was at his side. He put a hand on Herman's arm and asked him, "Why no?"

Herman's response was quick. "Future is now. Do not forget what is new and should be developed! We must think ahead!" Herman was through with speaking and made that clear. He closed his eyes and leaned back on the chair. A cloud passed by the sunny window enveloping Herman in its shadow. Then Herman revived, the sun returned, and all was as before.

This whole scene energized the family. Some were asking, "What does he mean?" Others urged Willie to take him out of the room to recover. Frank had thought no further than peacetime use and he was at a loss for words.

Only Willie and his father grasped the implications of Herman's message. Herman had seen German power first hand. Not the materials in use but the research behind them. It was not the time to look ahead in politics,

America wanted a "return to normalcy" and as much isolation from European challenges as possible. But that might be a mistake and that was Herman's message.

Eva was still trying to see if Women's Suffrage would be discussed. Emilia and Elise were totally immersed in Herman's speech, and each person present felt compelled to add to the general confusion. Eva nodded to her bloc and began to collect her thoughts. Augusta, Gertrud and husbands leaned towards the matriarch, ready for orders.

And then Elise slipped to the floor and lost her breakfast before them all.

Chapter 6

The Spanish Flu

"Well," sighed Willie, "It was not stress. I did think Elise had the serenity to accept the critics that came to find faults in Frank's plan. But now, Louisa, we will tread water until she is well again."

Louisa responded with heat, "Indeed we will not. She will be well enough in a month and all will be ready for her entry on the stage. Believe me Willie; this will give her a reason to get better quickly. And, if not, we will locate another to act as leader. I will tell her that as soon as she can understand what I am saying!"

"You absolutely amaze me with your dedication, Louisa." Willie admired his wife but had no idea of the depth of her commitment. As yet he had not equated this zeal with the treatment of her mother, now gone and even more potent in Louisa's mind. "You will wait until she can sit up? It is hard to take such information lying down."

"I am not a monster, Willie. You don't know how strongly Elise feels about the German community. And, I am happy to say, about other women as well." Louisa spoke softly but clearly.

The Melting Pot: 1919-1939

"Where is she now? Frank leaves next week, should you be taking charge of the home fires there? I can manage with Emilia and Wilhelm, excuse me, William. And I can help with Herman as well." Willie looked to Louisa waiting to see what she had already planned.

"Willie, I have talked to Frank once again. He was truly stressed and worried about Elise and the children. We have sorted it out. Elise will go to Emilia and William's home. Herman has a large room and it will become the nursing unit with curtains to divide it. Emilia is more than willing to be nurse to her two children. If not for the cause, I do believe she is delighted to have her children home."

"And the little ones? Can you leave them alone with only the nanny? That will surely worry Elise." Willie was not truly up on what was necessary for the care of three young children but he had met the nanny who was pleasant but a bit too flexible.

Louisa hesitated in fact she hesitated several times. "Willie, in the face of this problem we, that is, Frank and I have come to a solution that seems appropriate. At least both grandmothers think so. Frank's mother will move her grandchildren into her home in Avondale, with their nanny. Just until Elise if better. Her house is large and mostly empty of people. It is a good solution."

"Mein Gott!" Willie was astounded. "If anything will speed Elise's recovery it is this. Or it might kill her quickly. Do you have to tell her?"

"When she is firmly on the road to recovery we will. Now she is not in shape to hear our plan but she will approve. It does not change Frank's move, Eva loves the grandchildren, and Eva has not enough to do at home. If anything, Eva's daughters and their husbands will feel at peace if only for a few weeks."

"And Emilia? Is she up to this new challenge? I know she has become recognized as an authority on all things related to maternity matters, but the flu?" Willie respected his mother and was amazed that she had become totally immersed in nursing, the career she longed to discard when she married.

Louisa smiled. "You forget. Your mother has worked with flu patients in Germany where supplies and help were truly lacking. She is now assigned to the maternity wing at the hospital, ensuring no prospective or recent mother is exposed. Of course, she will have to give up her hospital visits until Elise is well. Emilia's knowledge is probably better than anyone else. And she wants to do this."

The move of Elise to her parent's home was completed that night. Frank continued to pack for his own move. Emilia and Eva prepared for the weeks ahead, glad to be able to help. And Herman had a roommate. When Elise was settled into the second hospital bed brought to the house, Herman spoke.

"Welcome home, Elise."

Influenza was another sad event near the close of World War I. The newspapers downplayed the spread of the disease in Germany, France, the UK and US to suppress fear. Instead, it was reported for neutral Spain, giving it the name Spanish Flu as a result. In this pandemic, the usual pattern targeting the very young and elderly was reversed with most of the fatalities being young adults between 20 and 40. Of pregnant women who survived, most lost the child. It is also confirmed a mortality rate in Germany higher than in Britain or France.

Both Elise and Herman had been in Germany in 1918. Both had been in the hospital in Canada, filled with soldiers returning from the continent. And they had spent much time in close quarters as Louis drove them home to Cincinnati. These markers were obvious. On the other side, Emilia who had also been in Germany had the training and mentoring of many Red Cross nurses as she volunteered in hospitals there. On arriving home, Emilia brought the expertise of those nurses, which often exceeded the speculation of doctors, to the hospitals of Cincinnati. She was as close to an expert in the treatment of flu as possible and she made it possible for her children to be treated at home.

Early on, Elise had a headache that she ascribed to Frank's news and his reluctance to share it. She had a sore throat, which she ascribed to travel and change of temperature in the past months. And in general she felt like resting instead of picking up where she had interrupted her life at home. By the time she was brought to her parent's home she had a high fever, a swelling of the throat, and vomiting. Herman had those symptoms and more on the trip back from Canada. Emilia calmly looked at the room, ordered pails and pans, basins and washcloths, pitchers of water. She was ready for the battle and the recovery.

Chapter 7

Recovery

Elise occupied a hospital bed adjacent to Herman's, separated by a canvas curtain on a large rod holder borrowed from the hospital where Emilia volunteered her services. A day maid and a night watch were organized to keep constant checks on the two patients. Emilia had seen some victims take sudden dips that resulted in death. This would not happen to Elise and Herman. It was clear to her that Herman's problems were more than his head injury, he had brought the disease from France and carried it back to the hospitals in Canada where Elise spent hours searching for him.

Her house was close to Elise and Frank's. It had been easy to take one of the guest rooms freed after Willie's departure and turn it into an emergency care space. Aside from the two maids who cleaned every surface often, two nurses were on duty, each taking a shift. Whenever possible, Emilia was there as well.

"Elise, Elise, wake-up!" Herman had been watching her for the last few days; sure she knew he was there. He called her often without response but this time, Elise opened her eyes.

"Where are we Herman? Are we still in Canada?"

"No Elise. We are in our mother's guest room and we will be well again. If you remember Canada it will just take time to recall everything you ever knew."

The day maid was removing the signs of the past night. Buckets were changed, water replaced, dishes and cups put in baskets. At first she was frightened by the two talkers, it was like being alone in the room before but now she had an audience. "I will tell your mother you need her!" The maid spoke in German, and then Elise was sure she was in her mother's house. The maid disappeared.

"Well, Herman, I am glad to have someone to talk to. Can you tell me what happened and why we are sharing the old nursery?" Elise looked over at Herman. The curtain had been pulled open and she could see his dark hair, a small bit of plaster on his forehead and a hand reaching out for hers. "Are we sick? Shell-chocked? At war? Why am I here?"

Herman smiled and touched her hand. "Just like the old days! You are asking questions and I have to answer. I believe, from what I hear, that we have flu. You were the dramatic one, ruining Frank's big moment and an oriental carpet. What was Frank talking about anyway?"

No answer from Elise. Then, tentatively, "I am not sure. Where is he?"

"I have not seen Frank for all the time I've been here. Certainly not recently but I can't be sure. Do you think he is afraid of the flu? Emilia is really the only one who steadily attends us along with an army of maids and nurses."

Elise was diverted by a need for her handkerchief. She didn't find it and realized the toweling near us had been left for that purpose. Of course Emilia would have all the details of the sick room in perfect shape.

Over the next week, Elise and Herman had time to reconnect as brother and sister, not lost and found. Herman asked for Louis. It was Louis, Sonia's brother and Frank's chauffeur, who brought him back to Cincinnati, attending to him in the car, helping him to eat and relieve himself, administering the medications that the hospital packed with him when they left. Herman was sure he had contributed to the spread of flu not only to Elise but also to Louis. He had not. For the rest of that day, Herman was content.

The next morning he woke early but found Elise sitting on the edge of her bed. "I feel much better today. I will try to stand now." And she did without any difficulty. Herman faced her from his own bed, and, slowly, stood. It was a heady moment, a statement of survival for each of them.

They were both asleep again when Emilia came in with the breakfast. She knew the corner was turned and left them sleeping.

Later that week Elise and Herman were talking in more general terms about the life that had returned. Herman was diffident but he wanted to know. "Elise, are you happy? You know what I mean. Is your life where you want it to be?"

The Melting Pot: 1919-1939

Elise slowly shook her head in a definitive no. The hair was still blonde and it had grown considerably. Her pale skin seemed as usual and the girl she had been was back, just for now. "Herman, there is still something missing. I thought, once a long while ago, that is might be a man to really love. That was not it."

"You need your own auto, Elise! That would give you true freedom!" Herman felt that anything mechanical, especially a means of transportation, would cure any problem.

"No Herman. It has been very long since I believed that things could make me happy. Women long for more than a big house, fine clothes, and servants to order. We need a place of our own in the world. Frank wants badly to be recognized. I do as well and I want all women to have the same recognition. It is our time."

"What are you talking about? You all seem to dominate whomever you meet. Look at what is happening in this family? Power is not happiness either! Elise, don't tell me any more today, I need to rest! What is that noise?" Herman pulled up his blanket and turned to the door.

The sound of children filled the room and Elise and Frank's small replicas entered bearing gifts.

William Frederick and Eva Emilia were holding hands. Grandmother Emilia grasped Max. He immediately tried to escape to go to his mother but Emilia had determined on a visual visit only. The hand that didn't clutch Max carried a cat carrier, and inside it was Olga, Elise's prized cat. It was a full visit of loved ones and it would be soon over.

The older children were shy and stood quietly, looking at the ceiling and not the patients. At last Elise called out, "Children I am fine! We must be careful that you do not catch any germs from me or Uncle Herman but we will save all our kisses for you!"

This seemed a frightening thought to William Frederick and Eva Emilia. Young Max tried one more escape move and then turned to leave. Emilia whispered, "Wave good-by, children, we will come back." And then the visitors left.

Elise called out, "Wait! Tell me when Frank will come!" She heard only a loud meow and they were gone.

"Good Grief. That was an ordeal for us all. Why does Mama feel the need to offer constant surprises?" Herman felt he had been a bad host. In fact, he had seen the children only once since his return and did not recognize them at all.

Elise laughed. "Herman, this is good news. If we were about to die Mama would never have brought them here." A pause. "I wonder that Frank did not come. I will ask when she returns."

"And now the cleaning crew is here." Herman shook his head in despair. In truth, he liked the two young women Emilia had hired.

Greta and Angelika had come to Cincinnati through various contacts, spoke little English, and had no close family. Their arrival was another surprise that Elise had managed while in Germany. The sisters had lost their immediate family and had a distant relative in Cincinnati who would sponsor their entry. Their Jewish faith made it a good decision even in 1914. The job of nurse/maid had not been planned but it was working well. The most amazing part was to hear Herman speak to them in German. It seemed that his head had not been as emptied as his family feared.

Elise suddenly asked, "Ladies, how much are you paid for this work? Where are you living?" There was an embarrassed silence. Then Angelika revealed that she did not know. Their "salary" went directly to the family where they were living at present. The uncle who had sponsored their entry could not offer them a home but had found a placement that seemed acceptable.

Elise felt that she had received a message from above. Her health was improving, her children were fine, and she had been given a task. "Herman, I would guess our Mama has excluded Louisa from the sick room so we would not be disturbed. I must see her to find out how our project is going. We need more than the vote on our agenda. We have virtual slavery in our midst."

Elise lay back to rest, the two girls left the room, and Herman said, "Of course." He hoped that Elise would not turn those lovely women into strident protesters with banners and posters in their delicate hands.

That night was restless for both. Elise was anxious about home, her children, the vote, and Frank. He had never properly explained his function in Washington or when he would be leaving Ohio. Herman had visions of Angelika in his mind. He wondered how her dark hair would look freed from the turban his grandmother had improvised. She needed saving. She needed him.

Jean Romano

When Emilia came with the day maids and breakfast she was pleased to see them both sitting up in their beds. Someone had raised the heads of the beds so that they no longer lay flat and unresponsive. This was the only thing that could please Emilia at the moment. She had done her part with her own talents but she was unable to control Eva, the grandmother who had recently moved the three children to her own home. And now, Emilia must tell Elise that the children were back with Eva in the big and empty house in Avondale.

Elise took the news well. On the outside, her flushed face indicated a return to good health. In a steady voice Elise stated as fact, "This move will end immediately and I am going home this afternoon to make all the arrangements. I will take Angelika and Greta with me for extra help. There is plenty of room for them with me and I will pay their salary face to face."

In truth, Elise did not hold any ill will towards Eva; it seemed the best alternative to leaving the children with the Nanny even if they were in their own home. Frank was in Washington. Elise was assured that he looked in and whispered, "I love you, good-bye." It didn't seem quite enough to Elise but of course the flu gave him a good reason to leave so abruptly.

The Clifton house was in good order and the children resettled in the nursery by teatime. It wasn't until the next day that Elise discovered that grandmother Eva had not moved the two older children to the Fairview-Clifton German Language School. Both of Elise's brothers had attended that school and it was her intention that her children would also be part of it as soon as possible. She had decided the time should be now when all was back to normal.

The Fairview-Clifton German Language School was founded in 1888 at a time when German was the largest single ethnic group in America, drawing immigrants from the Palatinates of Germany, Switzerland, and Austria-Hungary. Pennsylvania had the largest number but Ohio was close. The emphasis on academics was intense at this school for both boys and girls. Elise had looked at the books brought home by Willie and Herman and still felt a twinge of envy when she compared her learning materials to theirs. This would not happen to Eva Emilia.

What had happened now was no fault of Eva's. Eva sat with her daughter-in-law and explained why, when, and what passed while she was away. When America entered the War in spring, 1917, a Department of Education, formed at the Federal level, allowed the use of federal funds to States using English only. By 1919, the State of Ohio, and others, banned the teaching of German in private or public schools. The German Language School was not in operation.

Elise accepted this explanation with grace. She spoke to an empty room. "The ban will be lifted soon and then I can decide. Eva has returned the children to Clifton Avenue. The household is back to normal."

Eva no longer seemed the dragon of yore. Elise knew she had tried to follow her wishes. At that very moment she pledged to respect and love her mother-in-law in much the same way she had made a vow to accept Frank years ago. It might be easier to accomplish with Eva.

Elise's next step was to contact Louisa. What had happened and what was coming regarding the organization? It surely hadn't stopped because of my absence thought Elise. Eva's news had shaken her. What else was in the process of change? She would find out shortly.

Chapter 8

Emilia and William

Emilia had good news for William when they were settled at the dinner table that night. "Elise is home. The three children are home. Greta and Angelika will live in and provide all the help needed with child care. They will receive pay. William, life is good!"

"Who are the children you speak of, Emilia, and why are they with Elise?"

This was not the happy moment Emilia envisioned. She was glad that Herman had not felt ready to join them for dinner. She knew he was mourning the loss of Angelika if not Greta. "They are Elise and Frank's children, William, you are the grandfather of all three." Emilia said this lightly but her heart was as heavy as a Krupp cannon. William was forgetting those closest to him and she knew he couldn't carry on in the factory much longer.

There had been some recent conversations that were on her mind. Now she would have to talk to Frank, who was far away, or who else? She made a note to see Louisa the next day to find a way to discuss this with Willie.

Since Elise's marriage, Emilia had built a life of her own based on both her duties as a wife and mother and a person with much to offer her new homeland. She walked softly and was truly astonished when she realized that Elise envied her.

"Why on earth would you feel that particular emotion my dear daughter!" Emilia faced Elise on the ship carrying them to Germany, months past.

"Because, dear mother, you have been trained to perform a special function needed by many. I have not."

Emilia thought back to her days as a nurse in a Maternity Hospital for the wealthy families of Dusseldorf. At that time she felt as low as possible. In the social order there, she was no more than a trained servant to be paid for services and quickly forgotten. The patients who came early, gave birth, recovered and prepared to leave loved Emilia. They gave her presents and kisses. And after they left for home, they missed her not at all. She had met some on the streets of the city, usually while walking home. They would pass in their carriages without a wave or smile.

"Perhaps you are right, Elise, and I was meant to leave my home, cross the ocean and find a place where I could be of use. I care so much for the mothers who are poor wherever they live. They have so little hope for their children's future. Each new baby is a burden, not a joy. And I feel even more sorrow for the poor women who try to stop a new baby's birth because they have no hope at all. Perhaps, Elise, your project and mine will come together at some point for the good of many."

This short talk was not referred to again until much later but neither mother or daughter forgot it. The complex problems of poverty touched everyone whether they accepted the fact or not.

At this moment, Emilia was consumed with the issue of William. All the nursing skills she learned or taught herself, all the nursing skills in the world were ineffectual. She had attributed William's lapses to old age even though she was a bit older than he. In-group meetings he was silent more often than not but this had always been his way. When asked a question he would often change the subject, his seat, or the room he occupied. He had found ways to cope with his inability to understand. Emilia wondered now if he knew who she was.

This had been the topic Emilia anticipated but Elise had not. Her reason for seeking out Elise was William, husband to Emilia, father to Elise, grand=father to her three children, and advisor/partner with Frank. William had not been the same since Herman decided to stay in Germany, so many years ago. He began to lose his way through a story, and then a sentence. Willie's accident was a severe blow but it did not affect his faith in Willie's recovery as long as his brain was strong. But with Herman, he was afraid to explore just what was in his mind. Had Herman truly loved his time in the German Air Force? Did he want to return? William did not want to know but the thought never left him. In the end, he found it easier to forget what had happened and even to forget Herman.

When Emilia returned home with her brother, William asked, "Who is that young man with Elise?"

Emilia laughed and everyone decided William was making a joke. With Emilia's help, few realized that there was no joke and life was about to become all too real.

Emilia noticed his inability to focus or to give her orders as he had since their marriage. In truth, she gave orders throughout the day to keep him on course. And last week, when she had not the time to give, a group from the factory came to see her. The news was not good. They were concerned that William was often unaware of what was happening and what needed to happen. "Exactly how old is William?" This was asked respectfully but the ominous tone was present as well.

"It is not age." Emilia said this firmly. "The stress of our son's injuries during the war, the need for retooling the factory, and now the illness of both our daughter and son with flu has been severe. He is old but quite in touch with everything and everyone. I believe he needs a short time to rest and recover."

"What a good idea! We will rearrange our duties so that he can feel relief from the pressure of the job. We will stay in touch with you." The representative mediator thought of the lightness of touch that would be used. As far as they all were concerned, William was gone. But not forgotten. The company was partly owned by his family through his own investments and through Frank's. One step at a time.

Emilia decided not to speak to Frank before he left. It was clear that he would leave no matter what came up at home. Fine. The factory administrators would cover long enough for her to discuss this with Willie. It might be possible to bring in Augusta's husband who seemed more competent than Gertrud's. As she and William walked towards Elise's house, her mind was as shaky as his.

It was time to tell Elise. Through their time together on the boat to and from Germany she had let the matter rest. Once there they were far too busy to consider a problem as frivolous as senility. Emilia decided to have William present to avoid all possibility that Elise would not believe her. She planned to discuss the children's education and she knew William still considered Elise a visitor, not a daughter. It should not be long before Elise understood.

They climbed the stairs of the front porch. "Where are we, Emilia?" William was comfortable at home and at work. Nowhere else.

"This is Elise's home, William. We are paying our daughter a visit." Emilia wasn't sure of the next question. It didn't disappoint.

"When did we acquire a daughter?" William looked directly at her face to be sure he had her full attention.

And then Emilia rang the bell.

William behaved perfectly for the hour they spent taking tea with Emilia's friend, Elise. When they left, Elise took her mother's arm and said sweetly, "So good of you to visit. I will call on you tomorrow after lunch."

"I am so pleased to meet you," William bowed as a true gentleman should. "Emilia has spoken of you often and I looked forward to this visit."

Chapter 9

Mother and Daughter Confer

Emilia opened the door wide, as if encouraging Herman to leap out of bed and leave for an engagement. "I am so glad to see you," Herman really meant this, he had been alone long enough. Since Angelika and Greta had departed to live with Elise and the children, life had been depressing.

"I am in need of clothing. These hospital gowns you brought are out of style, Mama, can you bring me something to wear?" And it was true. The hospital gowns did not encourage socializing.

Elise determined to check Frank's wardrobe for anything close to suitable. There was a box of college clothes that would most likely fit Herman and they were closer to the current dress code than the suits Frank had been wearing lately. "Don't worry Herman. At the least I can dress you well enough to go shopping. At best, you will be invited for dinner some night soon. Louis will pick you up, he has been asking for you for weeks."

Elise kissed Herman, took her mother's arm, and they left the sick room. It would be Elise's last visit to Herman in that room. He was ready to move into the small back bedroom he occupied as a boy.

Emilia looked at her daughter with pride. Her inability to create a sampler in Finishing School was forgotten. She would follow her daughter's lead now, sure that her own goals would be incorporated. Emilia knew her own days would be devoted to William. He often was lost in his own home, a few steps outside the house and he was completely at sea. So far, she had managed to keep the seriousness of their plight a secret from most of the family. She told William that he was now retired and could live like a gentleman of leisure. He seemed comfortable with that explanation. Tonight a smaller family get-together would bring up the many issues to be addressed.

They were more than equal now. William had been the sturdy and fulsome man of industry and Emilia the small and undistinguished nurse. Both had lost height and weight but Emilia moved easily and William walked like a blind man searching for each step. The family would know the full extent of their father's decline this very day.

And so they would meet at Emilia and William's house. Willie would be there tonight after spending the day at the factory. He intended to check the books first, worried that the financial necessities had been short-changed. Not so. All the men at F & B had filled in to keep the business on even keel. The situation was beyond their expertise. They needed a mechanical engineer to retool and an economist to determine what to retool for – what were the products needed now? Who would hold the tiller? Perhaps it could be a joint effort.

Elise would be present that night. Even Herman would attend the family conference. She assured her mother that it would be sorted out and she had nothing to worry about. Before she left she brought up one more concern. "Before our lives are completely smothered in business, I want your opinion and your help on my own goals. Mama, I am serious about the women's vote and how to make it an informed vote. I am serious about identifying the issues we should fight for now. Can you help me?"

"Yes, Elise. These concerns will now be yours. Much is on the table and ignored by politicians. It will be up to women to bring new problems to the people for votes. In the hospital I have noted that since the army has been returning our soldiers, women have lost jobs they held for the past two years. Family finances have slowly improved as the men resume their jobs. For one, men receive better pay than women. But some women are left supporting children with no wages, even the lowest, as their husbands did not return. They need help. Another problem is especially difficult."

Emilia sat down. Emilia did not know how to start the next part of the discussion. "Many women, Elise, are desperate. Some do have husbands who came home ill from being gassed in the trenches, ill with flu, and just worn beyond repair. They cannot be breadwinners now and so there is no bread in their households. And still, human nature requires love and so there have been a few pregnancies. The women attempt abortions on their own and many die, leaving both husband and children already on earth and needing food and shelter. There must be help for these families."

This had never occurred to Elise, and, she was sure no one else in her particular social set was aware of the issues. All she knew grieved when a child died or was still born as her second had been. All efforts had been to protect life. And in some cases, abortions were arranged with physicians who were competent and discrete. This was a different picture. "When does new life mean suffering for those already here?" Elise looked at her mother with respect. She had left Over the Rhine behind her and lost a bit of the humanity that motivated her in the past.

"You are right. We will discuss this in committee first. Would you be willing to advise us on how to address the issue? I would imagine the church would also have ideas or solutions."

"Yes, Elise. I will help in any way I can."

The two parted with a quick embrace. Both giving the message and receiving it had not been easy. Emilia and William remained in the Catholic faith, raising their children in the local parish. One strong connection to the other German community was the church. When Elise married, Eva ensured her switch to the Lutherans. To Elise it was not a difficult leap, as her faith did not depend on which church she attended. She did have belief in her mother's ability to guide them through some of the issues just described.

Meetings had continued while Elise recovered. Louisa

brought her into the discussions and she was anxious to reach out to the immigrant women. They had been ignored until Elise joined the team. It was apparent that Emilia was very aware of the poverty and concerns of these women and more than willing to help them. The weather was turning away from winter and it was a good time for the three women to plan a meeting. They would draft at speech together.

Chapter 10

Who Will Have The Vote?

Louisa attended all meetings held by the local branch of The Ohio Women's Suffrage Association. Willie felt she was better employed at his side; her skills at reading and understanding the books he brought in from the University amazed him. Still, he could see the advantage of the women's vote. "God knows, the men have not done very well with their power." Willie and Louisa made a special couple. His background in mathematics, economics and industrial growth was aided by her English skills and writing ability.

Willie signed and sat down to listen to Louisa. He knew the long= range goal was State ratification of the 19th amendment that had moved to the back burner during the war. It was expected that women would be eligible to vote in the 1920 elections. With help, Ohio would be among the first States to vote for ratification.

Willie talked to Louisa about the need for all women to come together. Louisa responded, "that is not possible, Willie, and we cannot sit back and wait for such a miracle to happen. We will unite as best we can when it is time."

Willie was correct and he had noticed that three different organizations were active for women's suffrage in Cincinnati. There was the Central Suffrage Committee, The 20th Century Club, and the Susan B. Anthony Club. This bothered Willie. The suffrage rallies were often attended by more men than ladies. "Are they still looking towards men as their leaders? Is there a human need for the Alpha male, and none for the Queen Bee?" Willie felt he was ahead of the times and left the discussions to the women when they next met.

There were many dissensions in the ranks. Louisa was still shocked that some were opposed to black women being included in the movement. The addition of their vote could swing some states, districts, or cities towards legislation that was unwanted in the southern states. Louisa had been thinking above the concrete, concerned only with the rights of all citizens. Cincinnati had been a primary stop during the days of the Underground Railway, she thought that ensured a liberal take on the acceptance of Black Americans. The political reality of a voting bloc had not registered.

Louisa created a list of problems to discuss with Elise when the time seemed ripe. Willie cautioned her to be slow and sure that Elise was fully alert before bringing her into the fray once again. And it was going to be a battle for control at all levels.

Louisa adjusted her bun. No bobs for her, she was to remain the link between past and present. "And Elise's bob was hygienic, not fashion dictated." That closed her thoughts on appearance for the day. She had other concerns.

The Melting Pot: 1919-1939

A small committee meeting was scheduled at Emilia and William's house so that Emilia could attend. The seven ladies who came could use the dining room table. A Rookwood fireplace was at one end of the long room, and pocket doors faced it at the other end. The table was chosen to seat fourteen. Emilia determined the number of chairs by counting those who would be with them for special dates. Today the visitors sat at one end, facing the door to the foyer. Windows filled one side, doors to the breakfast and sitting room were on the other side. The room was meant for conversation and the women were ready.

Louisa had copies of the current goals for each member. First was the specific notation of the organization as non- partisan. Even though it appeared Ohio would be presenting a conservative candidate for President in the next election, the group would press only for a considered vote on issues, not a specific party. Information would be non-partisan as well and researched to give meaning to the ballot. And the ballot would be available for scrutiny before the election. The group was doing well. Louisa was tempted to send them home before more difficult topics arose.

Of course, that was not to happen. One of the ladies who had been driven in from Avondale asked if the group intended to include all women or only those from the German-American district. Over the Rhine still flourished and it had its share of women with complicated lives. The biggest issue there, however, was Prohibition. This was discussed with delicacy as most present had found their families unaffected by the ban on liquor. "Let's move on to another issue," said the lady from Avondale. "I know the work done by our hostesses in bringing many German-American families to citizenship. It is commendable. They will surely vote and be open to receiving information, especially the women. What about other areas in the city? Are they off bounds to this group?"

"Certainly not," Louisa was afire. "We must recognize that women are not a *bloc* who vote and believe as one. This message was now internalized. But if we are fighting for each woman to have a voice, all should be part of our effort. This means that we contact the women in the area called Appalachia. They are working women as well as wives and mothers. And we must include the black women who work and need a voice. If we are sincere in what we do, we reach out to all and in 100 years we will have left a legacy."

Elise rose and put an arm around Louisa. "Friend, you have said it all." None spoke for a few moments but then, instead of words, they began to clap hands. One stood and said simply and with feeling, "To the Sisterhood!"

The next election would replace President Woodrow Wilson. He had finally come to the support of Women's Suffrage nut would no longer be the leader of the government. Change was in the air. The goal now had to be getting information on registration and the ballot out to all. And there were good men, like Willie, who would help extend their reach.

The next meeting of the smaller group would plan for the larger meeting ahead. Aside from the vote itself, the issues of concern were: unions, labor laws, minimum wages, and the work environment. Many of the women they hoped to reach worked outside the home in some capacity from laundries to factories. When the men came home from the war, many lost their jobs and they were urged to "give their job to a man." Yet some of the women were the sole support of the family. For businesses, women were the cheapest labor. And children worked as well. The goal would be a Women's Bureau in the Department of Labor. And labor laws specific to children. Each solution produced another point of concern.

Elise awoke. "Education of women must be equal to that of men. We lose the abilities of half our population by promoting embroidery over mathematics. No discrimination by gender!" This was the first public statement Elise had made that was unrelated to citizenship. More clapping.

It was decided that Elise should be the lead speaker at the large rally in late summer. And a time and place were selected. Elise smiled bravely pretending the choice was agreeable. Despite her recent foray into speaking her opinion, she was unsure of her ability to hold forth before the multitudes. Nevertheless, all came to pass later that summer.

"Willkommen!" Elise chose her first word carefully and the chattering audience quickly came to attention. Every seat in the meeting room was taken and a few women stood along the wall at the back of the room. Eventually someone would remember the capacity limits but for now the group had been called to order. When

Jean Romano

Elise looked out at the sea of femininity her heart swelled, her brow grew damp, and the papers in her hands rustled like birds in flight. With all her heart she wanted to speak well to these women. In part of her heart she knew her ability to speak had never been tested.

Her speech was delivered in German until she reached the halfway point. Her explanation of where the law stood now, the ambiguity of the 14th amendment and the efforts to ensure the right of women to vote. The place of this community in the fight had been presented to enlist a cadre of activists.

And then a voice called out, "Speak English!"

There was silence and then clapping. The voice identified itself as Frau Schindler and she stood and continued to speak as the noise diminished. "We are here to exercise our full rights as citizens. Frau Freimarck, you have helped many of us become citizens and now we are ready to work for our country to make women equal partners in governing this country. We are no longer German-Americans, we are Americans. We need to hear the plans and assignments in English to fully integrate our effort with our English speaking sisters."

Frau Schindler sat to silence and then even louder applause than before. Elise was shocked, surprised, and overcome with a kind of shame. She had assumed her role as the spokesperson for the German community was necessary. Now she realized her mistake. Never again would she decide that these women should be treated differently and that they needed her to speak for them. She might lead now but other leaders were ready and able.

Frau Schindler rose again. "Now, Frau Freimarck, please continue."

Elise looked to Louisa for support. Louisa moved to the poster board to display the first points of action approved by the Hamilton County Committee. They were written in English. OUSA or Ohio Women's Suffrage Association started as part of the countrywide reaction against the 14th amendment. That amendment enfranchised black men but not women of any color. The word "male" was writ large within the wording. OUSA was not State wide but it was organized and determined to campaign for a State constitutional change. This goal was elusive before World War I but the role of women during wartime had given new strength to their fight.

Looking back, women's suffrage was won state by state. The Cincinnati organization was one of the oldest in existence. The women were not a unified group in Ohio, three organizations had been formed: Bettie Wilson was President of the Hamilton County Association in Cincinnati. She would be the guide for Elise and Louisa. The group sought reform regardless of political affiliation and fought for laws, not specific people.

The League goals were clear and the reason why Elise and Louisa felt the task worthy. Women would vote but they would act as an informed electorate. Until the 19th amendment came to life, they would work towards its passage. After that milestone, they would continue their goal of providing information about issues at hand.

Louisa distributed copies of the 19th amendment through the audience. There were not enough, but they were shared. Section I. was read. Emphasis on the phrase "All persons born or naturalized in the United States, and subject to the jurisdiction thereof, are citizens of the United States and of the State wherein they reside. No State shall make or enforce any law which shall abridge the privileges or immunities of citizens of the United States." There were some puzzled expressions on the faces Elise could see.

"Let me move on to Section 2." Elise changed her course and got to the point. "In this Section, the right to vote is denied to male inhabitants who have participated in rebellion or other crimes. I am shortening this Section but we have brought full copies to distribute when you leave. It is the use of the word male that is your trigger. Females are not included in the right to vote by virtue of their gender. It is assumed that they do not have the intellect to vote. It is predicted that they never will. How speak you, women of Ohio and the USA?" And speak they did. The first organizational meeting was a success.

Nominations for a working committee were requested and the two organizers left with the names of possible candidates.

Elise and Louisa wanted to expand their message far beyond the right to vote. Small steps were determined best. As the room cleared, several women remained behind to talk to them. Elise recognized Angelika and Greta on the fringe and motioned them closer. The two young women seemed frightened but determined to join the group. Elise asked, "Did you understand what was said?" "No, responded Angelika, but Herman will explain it to us later."

A light turned on. Herman's recovery was linked to a purpose. He was aware of his ability to relate to the two sisters. "Is it just nobility of spirit?" Elise quickly dismissed that idea. "I will try to find an answer and, I will try to find a way to involve Herman in the future. Women's Suffrage is in need of good men too."

This thought brought Frank into the picture. "What on earth is he doing now? His mother says nothing, my father says less, and Willie is avoiding me. Time to investigate with delicacy of course." Elise's head was swimming. Her first decision was to cut her hair. Then she would reset her schedule to include the status of Frank Freimarck.

Chapter 11

Two Stories

Elise turned to leave the meeting and was surprised to see Herman standing in the back of the hall. She was more surprised when she saw Angelika and Greta join him. "Well, Herman, I have always said a few good men are needed! You are more than welcome to join our crusade!"

"I have already been recruited, Elise. I believe you know these two ladies?"

Elise looked cross for just a moment. "I know them well, Herman, and trust they have left the children in good hands?" Both of the young women looked at Elise with confidence.

"The children are in school and will not be home for another hour. Do you recall we did tell you we would attend?" Greta seemed to feel the pressure more than her sister. Angelika who then added, "This meeting was scheduled for school hours so that mothers could come without a problem of childcare. And so our charges are cared for too!"

Elise was ashamed of herself. This had been a day where

she miscalculated everything important and finished by treating these two women as misbehaving youngsters. "Of course. Forgive me; my mind is overloaded with details. I am about to leave for a quiet walk home and a cup of tea. You have extra time if you wish it, I will be there when the children return." Elise left quickly with her customary reddened face.

Herman laughed. And then Greta and Angelika laughed with him. It was the easiest way to pass over the small awkwardness that shouldn't have happened. The three turned to leave but stopped to greet Louisa. She was happy to see Herman out and with company other than the immediate family. It had to be medicinal in a good way.

"Come to my place for your tea! You can use this little break before life continues. Will Louis drive us? Yes? Let's go now."

The three were soon in the tiny apartment of Louisa and Willie. Herman noted that it was the smallest room he had ever sat down in for tea. This bothered Louisa not at all. It was all they needed as Willie had an office space at the University and preferred working there. They took the opportunity to talk about Willie. It wasn't often that he was absent.

"How does his work go? I have heard rumors that he is taking on some of the duties of F & B as well." Herman opened the discussion, careful to give Louisa an easy topic if she chose not to discuss William. She did not.

"Willie is fine. He can do whatever he has to and he will. Never worry about your brother, Herman; he has been fine since you came home. You cannot imagine how hard it was for him during the years you were gone. There was enough blame to go around but Elise and Willie competed for the honor of being the one who doomed you to an early death. Your father suffered in silence but truly, he may have been the hardest hit by your disappearance.

Not one member of the family had attempted to ask him about his time in Germany. This was the first, and perhaps the last time he could explain some of it and include Greta and Angelika. He knew they were anxious to hear his story and he wanted them to hear it.

"Perfect timing. Tea and sympathy, Louisa, you are the perfect sister-in-law. Ladies, let me very briefly tell you what the last five years meant to me. Did you know that I not only volunteered to stay in Germany, I begged to stay in Germany after Willie and I finished our short visit with Frank's family. It had only taken me a few days to talk of my love of planes and flying and in a few more days I had the opportunity to learn about flying as part of the German Air Service. That would be the Die Fliegertruppen to you, Greta and Angelika. Our family in Germany were connected and I was allowed to enroll."

Angelika and Greta looked thoughtful. Greta said slowly, "Herman, you don't enroll in the German Army like a course in high school."

"You are so right, Greta! Too bad you didn't tell me that at the time! When I finished the 'course' of course, it was explained forcefully that I was trained and now part of an exciting part of history. And, I must admit, there was that piece to tempt me."

"There were three main parts to the aeronautics department then. I was assigned to the two-man observation planes and my partner and I became attached to a unit on the Western Front. The biggest problem at that time was determining a way to fire machine guns from fighter planes. I understand now that a French plane, manned by Roland Garros, was shot down, captured, and used by Fokker to learn how to synchronize the guns and propeller actions. I remained where I was, as an observer who reported artillery positions. Thank God. And thank God I was shot down before any reassignment could occur. I was not yet twenty years of age. My partner, my best friend, died in the wreckage. He was Jewish. May he rest in peace."

Louisa was quietly crying. "Do you know how happy this will make Willie? He has imagined the very worst for years. You must tell him yourself."

"It is right that I do this. Louisa, please tell him that he and I need to talk." Herman was misty too.

"Please." Greta took Angelika's hand. "It is time to tell our story. We lived in eastern Germany with our family for many generations. My grandfather was a cantor for our community. Until the end of the war, we were loyal to Germany. Indeed, our father was in the German army too, Herman. After a Treaty was signed with Russia, our lives were changed. Russia had lost. Through Revolution it is true. But when the Russian Jews began to come into Germany they were poor, uneducated, desperate people and they were not welcome. In short, Jews were not seen as part of the community any longer. And our father did not come home. Mother died of flu, or maybe grief. Cousins and other family left our town. And then we met your mother at the hospital where our mother died. She and Elise found a way to bring us here."

Another story and more tears. The meeting had been exciting but the two stories told in a quiet room over teacups were a fitting ending to a day of new beginnings. Herman stood and thanked Louisa. "This could only have happened in your house, in your presence. I will never forget this moment."

The two women stood. Louisa came to give each one a quick embrace and then opened the door for their departure. It was time Greta and Angelika went home to relieve Elise. William Frederick, Eva Emilia, and Max would be home and prepared to evade the disciplined behavior of the past five hours.

As they left, Louisa said with much feeling, "Greta and Angelika, the next time we meet for tea it will be time to hear your story in every detail."

The two young women left with mixed thoughts on sharing their story. Neither of them had any desire to relive the past or to elicit sympathy from those who did not see what had happened so far from home. It certainly would not be Louisa who heard their tale of woe. And it was over. The one thorn that still hurt was the loss of their religion. It would have been extremely hard to find a Temple in Cincinnati but they did not try. For now, they were grateful to be safe, fed, and housed in America.

Chapter 12

The Next Generation....

Eva was ready to move the children back to their mother. She was not happy on many fronts. For one, the slim and boyish look of Elise and Emilia bothered her deeply. She herself looked the proper Oma of a family, nicely padded and dressed to fit her curves. It was hard to be a widow and even more difficult to see her influence growing less each year.

Eva looked at the work of women's suffrage with a skeptical eye. This was surely not the way for her daughters or daughter-in-law to make their mark. There was still the Symphony after all. Or the Art Museum! Or simply running a household! Shopping! School visits! Entertaining!

Frank's disappearance was also a blow and she knew him well enough to realize he would need constant reassurance of his appeal to the ladies as a handsome man. Who would those ladies be? Few families had resettled in Washington but there would be women at work from laundresses to typists. Eva felt Frank had limited access to the cream of society by making the move.

Her thoughts moved on to her primary concern: Frank's children. She did not usually include Elise in these musings but from now on she would have to consider Elise as the parent in charge. And this was a critical time for William Frederick, Frank's son, the oldest and most talented boy in Eva's world. He was almost ready to move on to Walnut Hills High School, and if the testing and recommendations did not support his entry, Eva would have to unleash all her considerable power. She preferred not to be involved.

Augusta's son, Charles, was already attending Walnut Hills. The alternative would not be a disaster as there was a segregated school designed for black students and there would not be a question of racial mixing even if William Frederick had to attend the newly opened Withrow High. But to have Charles placed on a throne and Frank's son looking up to him? That would not do. Eva resolved to have William Frederick's teachers scheduled for an update on his achievement scores.

In fact, William Frederick was a good student. He inherited Frank's masculine stature and his mother's beauty. By the time he reached high school age, he discarded the William and was known only as Frederick, or Rick in his own age group. All of his teachers liked him for his manners and efforts to learn. Eva worried that they liked him too much and graded him accordingly. Elise knew that his love of reading was the reason, and maybe his devotion to Uncle Willie who spent time teaching him mathematical principles he didn't learn in school.

Frederick had dreams of being an inventor of things mechanical, things of the future.

His sister, named for the two grandmothers, was much the same. Elise watched her daughter with the concern Eva lavished on Frederick. Elise's girl would be educated in the same manner as her brothers. She would sew no sampler, serve no afternoon tea, or leave a calling card at the door of current social icons. And her friends would have the same goals: independence, education, and success in something unconnected to a kitchen.

Eva Emilia had two grandmothers who were polar opposites in their ambitions for their namesake. Eva saw her as a great social success. Emilia saw her as a potential doctor rising above the rank of nurse to the expertise Emilia long dreamed about since her own childhood.

Meanwhile, the city prepared its children with diligence. Two high schools were dedicated to academics. Walnut Hills and Withrow were both public schools preparing their students for University.

Cincinnati had a history of pre-school attendance and the three Freimarck children started at an early age. Max was newly enrolled and feeling full of himself at last. He spent his last nursery years with a nanny he did not like. School was his idea of heaven. Although Frederick asked him each day what he had learned in "Infant School", Max was sure he was smarter than his brother and sister combined. His mother told him so.

One concern unvoiced by Elise was the establishment of a segregated "black" school, fought for and defended by Jennie D. Porter. This educator deplored the lack of success by black students and planned to correct it by creating a system for black students that was administered and taught by black staff. So far, scores and other achievement indicators showed her strategy was making a difference for the good. Nevertheless, Elise felt that segregation was not a good thing in the army, in business, in sports, or in school and the quicker all were competing together the sooner the country would fulfill its potential. She was not in the majority but hoped the Women's Vote would move this issue in the right direction.

When summer vacation came, Elise would carefully assess the options. Her children would not be visiting train stations or fighting off rabid raccoons in the woodland behind their home. Her own childhood had been more exciting than she would allow her offspring, but there were many more opportunities for them as well. A tutor came to the house to keep the two oldest on task. The Freimarck membership in the Country Club assured them of access to golf, tennis and swimming. Max would be his mother's project.

School sports would be a great addition for Frederick. He had the same energy his uncles once had and less of an outlet. He played soccer with the local German team but now he could participate in baseball during school time. Elise was not in favor of football although Frank thought it the more manly sport. Nippert Stadium opened in 1915, home to the Cincinnati Bearcats. She saw the sport in action only once but that was enough. Elise worried about the effects of head butts and tackles.

For Eva Emilia, when her turn came, physical

education would serve until young ladies were offered more than golf, tennis, or swimming.

At the close of summer all was well. Frederick would attend Walnut Hills and wear long trousers at last. Eva Emilia would increase her studies to assure that she would join her brother in a few years. Max would be his mother's joy.

Eva was confident that Frank's sons would do better than cousin Charles, son of her daughter Augusta. He was an only child, spoiled by his mother and ignored by his father. Charles did not like sports. The other daughter, Gertrud, had produced three girls. Mary, Elizabeth and Jane were charming but their worth would be determined by whom they married. That was too far in the future for Eva to give thought to now. However, she might just look at the class lists to see the potential.

In all, the seven children at issue were launched with her help. Only time could tell what breeding would produce. Eva closed out her busy day with that in mind.

Part Two
The '20's

Chapter 13

Frank Arrives in Washington D.C.

Frank had kept close tabs on Elise and Herman, felt they were in good hands and was glad they were not his own. Illness was not one of his specialties. It was certain they would recover more quickly if he were gone. That concluded his virtual contact with family for the day.

He had found lodging in a converted house in Georgetown. It was now an apartment building, seeking to create a home away from home for new residents of the city who were part of the government in some way. The inhabitants were a lively crew of males, seeking entertainment, as well as career advancement, in various ways. The city had much to offer. Frank became a favorite partner for those looking for excitement. Most had families who stayed at home in their home States. They were all fairly anonymous, young enough to have ambitions not possible at home, and surrounded by the temptations Washington had in abundance.

"Has anyone seen Frank?" This was a query heard throughout the building.

All were open to the new lifestyle on display. The routines of wherever they originated were different. Music changed from the regal tones of the Symphony to the Jazz of Louie Armstrong. Frank found he preferred it. Prohibition was the law but not the reality. Ladies wore short dresses and rolled their stockings, often in public.

"I haven't felt this free since college! Washington has made me young again." Frank was not young but he fit into the city very well. In truth, his multitude of friends tripled the numbers he had at any stage of his school or business life to this point in time. Diversity of social class, education, and life goals made Frank a winner at last.

The biggest loss for Frank was the Cincinnati baseball team. Sports were his special interest. If the Reds made the World Series this season, and Frank was sure they would, his seat at the games held on Redland Field were confirmed through orders to Willie. Meanwhile, he could stay involved with the Washington Senators. He did not expect to divide his loyalty to the Reds but found he could adjust it to include attending games at National Park. He bought a radio as insurance.

Frank's small studio apartment was adequate and a good excuse for spending nights elsewhere. The Jazz clubs were growing and the music incredible. Duke Ellington and the Washingtonians, Ella Fitzgerald and more were available every night. Frank began his nightlife with friends from the apartment house but made many more each time he visited a new club or district in the city. He was as well known in the segregated U Street corridor as he was in his office. And when nothing was offered musically, there were enormous theaters showing movies at all hours. Frank was especially fond of Pola Negri and could sit through the same film several times.

Letters home were written each week: one to his mother, one to Willie, and a third note to Elise and their children. Frank was proud of this feat and hoped they wouldn't answer him too quickly.

He spent the days in his office. It was meant for serious work – it had no window to look out at the city. He studied the current laws and proposals coming in from home and abroad. By the end of the first few weeks Frank was well known in the Department of Labor and the Department of Commerce. His job was to align the present economy of America with the needs of Europe and, as a new player, parts of Asia. The many conversations he had with William Holtz prepared him for the process of retooling in industry, his talks with Willie had taught him how to finance this process. In the next ten years, Frank was sure America would become the powerhouse it was capable of being. He looked at an imaginary calendar. "That brings us to 1929 at the latest, and I will be ready to take advantage of this moment in history!"

And he, an American of German ancestry, would be one of the key players. It was a heady thought. President Wilson was in office but elections were already the topic of newspapers and radio broadcasters. The White House Correspondents and the Press Briefing Room in the West Wing were the main links between the public and the government. Frank made friendships in that group that were strong enough to get him an invitation to their Annual Dinner.

"What news today?" Frank stood in the crush of journalists waiting for a spokesman of the President to appear for their briefing.

"We are hoping for The Secretary of Labor to give us some news. The talk is about some good decisions on wages and hours. The strikes have stopped but nothing else has been accomplished."

This was not one of Frank's causes. He let the group push past him and he returned to his office. His own concern centered on the possible new federal income tax that would allow lowered tariffs and a final report from the War Industries Board. He and Willie discussed strategies at length. The last chance for a conversation ended badly. It finally dawned on Frank that although he applauded much of President Wilson's actions, including allowing the employment of Frank Freimarck, Wilson was more inclined to back the Republican's plank that would protect America from foreign competition. Willie, who should know better, wanted tariffs lowered as he saw them as a tax on consumers. For all of his University learning, Willie could be clueless on economic matters. Frank tucked this conclusion in the back of his mind.

The two tasks deemed most important after World War I focused on the revenue trend that needed regulation and the repair of economic damage from the war that caused purchasing on credit Frank's job was to work on the latter issue. It came down to ending barriers to world trade. This meant the lowering tariffs, the plan that Willie favored. He would think about that later. First issue was to assist the rebuilding of countries damaged by war, restarting peacetime industries, and setting some global standards for labor.

The rebuilding of Europe would be expensive. Frank mentioned to a journalist friend that Germany would be paying for that through reparations and it was expected that all would be well. This duly appeared in the press. In his heart, Frank felt sympathy for the German people. He had memorized a list of German debts and losses: it seemed endless. The list included mineral rights in Alsace-Lorraine, and administration of the Saar Basin by the League. Both of these items affected industrial recovery.

Frank decided to write to Willie and invite him to Washington for a visit. He needed a Professor (almost) to explain how a country losing one half of its iron supplies, two-fifths of its coal, and subject to a fixed debt for reparations of over five billion in the form of gold, ships, construction materials, coal, and commodities, could recover.

Willie received the letter and decided there was a better chance of moving Frank to his point of view in person. He talked to Louisa, then Elise, and finally Eva. He would make the trip.

Chapter 14

A Difference of Opinion

America was as divided as Willie and Frank on the direction to take for the next years. President Wilson had a stroke in early fall and although he planned to finish his term, the party would run a new Democrat candidate, the Republicans were ready with their candidate and a new President would be in office by 1921. The country was ready for a change. There had been race riots, strikes, and the "Red Scare", each episode alerting some part of the population to a concern that needed addressing.

Frank had entered Washington in the months preceding a national election. It appeared that "no foreign entanglements" would prevail but what did that mean? Frank followed the Republican view and was for imposing tariffs. He assured Willie in so many words.

"It is for the best. We do not want to compete with foreign goods. We want to export heavily to support the recovery of our allies in the war. America will grow stronger by helping them and it is to our advantage to have the balance of trade on our side." Frank saw no possible argument against his plan. His report would set it out in detail, hopefully with Willie's help.

Economists like Willie worried about the debt other countries owed America. Lending credit was virtually the only way America could send the materials and food needed in Europe before America entered the war. After America entered the war, the accumulation of debt from Europe continued, most of it by private investors. And now the war was ended. There was just so much that reparations could cover and so the debts from abroad continued to rise as interest payments were added.

Willie was careful. "If we raise tariffs higher, Frank, our former allies will be unable to pay. International trade is built on the competence and the diversity of resources, labor, climate and knowledge. We don't have a lock on all factors. If we allow other nations to rebuild we will have trade again. What is the alternative? Supply the needs of the world alone? If the countries in debt now cannot rebuild and establish themselves as players in the global economy, how will they pay for whatever we are selling? And think, we must rebuild our own economy for the future of our people as well as theirs. We need what they will produce and we need the money they will make by selling it."

If Willie was careful, Frank was thoughtful. "Your point is well taken but consider this. A new President will be listening to a very different drummer. I don't intend to leave Washington when Woodrow Wilson does."

"That is a different question. Your job now is to advise on the resurgence of International Trade. Take the long view, Frank, and you will find a more lasting success."

"Our largest business was with Germany. How does that a factor in for you? Willie, we are virtually on our own now and at the cusp of world domination. I like the feel of this."

Willie said only this. "Keep an open mind, do what you must now and then wait until after the election. Capitalism, Bolshevism, and Socialism are all theories and a case could be made for any of them. The problem is who you are trying to convince and how does any political theory work in a specific place and situation?"

This was definitely the moment to change the subject. "Frank, I came, in part, to tell you that your mother is not well. She is depending on Augusta and Gertrud while giving them enough advice to last throughout their lifetimes. Perhaps you can fit in a visit home?"

The change of subject did get attention and Frank promised Willie he would be in touch with those at home as soon as possible.

While they sat thinking their own thoughts a voice called from downstairs. "Frank, you are wanted on the telephone."

Frank came back to the room and slumped into a chair. "Willie, that was Augusta on the phone. Mama has died."

Willie offered condolences and apologized for not telling Frank of her illness much sooner. "She never complained and refused to let Emilia counsel her. We were all worried but didn't want to bother you without specific cause."

Frank expressed his thanks for Willie's sympathy and pulled out his suitcase. "I must go home and make arrangements. But first, I need to alert my supervisor that I will be gone for awhile. Willie, may I recommend you to this man? He is in the middle of the final report from this administration and will be left short-handed until I can return."

This was not the way Willie had planned the trip. He was fairly certain of the kind of advice Frank needed and doubtful if he would take it. As for the report, it was written by the Wilson Administration and most surely would align with his own views. And then, what does one say at this time to a brother-in-law? "Of course, Frank. I will keep your room in good shape for your return."

Frank's mention of the change of Presidents gave Willie a turn. He knew that his brother-in-law did not share his views on the role of government. Willie saw Wilson as close to perfection. He believed in the League of Nations and the importance of allies. Even more strongly, he believed that America was obligated to raise the standard of living for all its citizens. And the talk of "a return to normalcy" struck him as a very bad idea. But he came to Washington for Frank. His own views would be kept for another time.

There was a late train west that night and Frank was on it. In his bag he had a jar of Marmite that his mother had asked him to buy for her when he left home. Her last words to him might well have been "You will surely be able to find marmite in Washington!" He did buy it but his return home was not in time for her to enjoy the treat and the proof of his devotion.

Chapter 15

A Shuffle of the Deck

Every death changes the position of family members. Some are better consolers than others, and a few laggards finally enter the picture to pick up the slack in other ways. And so it was in Cincinnati, where some of the family had now lived for over forty years.

Frank's side of the family had brought capital and the ability to use it well. Elise's father had come to America with technical skills, honed at the Krupp Company that eventually made his uncle's factories lucrative. Despite World War I and the general hatred of the "Huns" the family had a secure place in America in the 1920's. It was the change in roles that was most notable.

Eva was buried with all the ceremony possible for the Lutheran Church. Attendance was at a record high with a great showing of black dresses, veils, suits, top hats and ties. The family members wore black bands on their sleeves. On the door of Eva's last home, a funeral wreath announced her passing to the neighborhood.

The eulogy, delivered by Frank, was a tribute to all of Eva's entire life, as many knew her only in her later years.

The Melting Pot: 1919-1939

It had been a long time since the family recognized her early efforts to assist the Jewish community in Germany. Many thought of her only as the perfect mother, mother-in-law and wife. Frank completed his part with thanks to the mother who had insisted on his education as a right of passage for her family. They would belong. It was clear to the audience that Frank was the chosen child: an athlete, a student, a businessman, and a participant in the American government. He thanked his mother for supporting him in all of his efforts and there were tears.

Augusta, Gertrud and their husbands behaved with dignity. It would take quite some time before the ladies realized they could make their own decisions. Frank already had plans for their well educated but not too busy husbands. They were trainable too, and they would have to become workingmen for now. Willie would help when he returned. Not the smallest thought was given to Herman. Neither did Frank give a thought to his own part in the workings of F & B of Cincinnati. Time to pass the torch.

Emilia and William attended the funeral. They stayed close to Elise, Willie, and Louisa. Emilia needed all the help she could get: William's memory loss increased daily to the point where he was lost in his own home. Taking him to mix with a crowd of sympathizers was an act of courage. The Freimarck children sat with the nanny. She was a black woman, chosen by Elise at one of the League meetings. She was outspoken, smart, and ready to educate herself. Elise was determined to help her move from her current position to one better suited to her intelligence.

Augusta's son, Charles, sat with his parents. In fact, he was Frank's heir, in Eva's mind. While her observations showed the academic dominance of Frank's children, Charles was most like Frank himself. A mother knows. Gertrud's three daughters, suitably dressed in black, sat quietly with their parents who recognized the more central role of Charles. Each one had a different reaction to Eva's passing but all performed their duty well.

Herman came with Emilia and William and managed to steer his father through the ceremony, the burial, and the refreshments afterwards. Herman had been the problem for some months and now he was part of the solution to a different kind of problem. Emilia's black dress and shawl made her look even sterner than usual. In fact, she was exhausted. If not for the help of Herman and the attendance of Greta and Angelika, she would not be walking let alone attending a funeral. Life had been exceedingly hard but she was coping and depending on Elise to provide support.

The day after the funeral there was a second family meeting. Again, all attended and the family lawyer read Eva's Last Will and Testament. Frank was to be Executor. Frank sat quietly thinking about this and by the end of the reading he had determined to schedule an appointment with the lawyer. It clearly stated that "if Frank is unable to act as Executor he will choose another with the advice of Attorney." That would be the first order of business tomorrow.

John Alden, Gertrud's husband, was a lawyer. Frank spoke to him as they left the reading. "John, I am going to ask you a favor. This is a family matter and I believe you are the right person to be involved."

John looked as if he disagreed with this statement but the next day he walked into the study with Frank close behind. They looked at each other and before a word was spoken John had accepted whatever was about to come. He wondered where his law school library had been stored: especially the volumes about Wills and Estates. When they left, with Frank's arm around his shoulders, John knew his days of leisure were over. There would be the settling of the Estate, the visit to Probate Court, the disposal of property and other minutia that would consume him for the next year. Moreover, Frank had hinted a further need for his services in the capacity of F & B's Firm Attorney.

Roger Taft enjoyed life, stayed in his own social set, was kind to his wife and child and wasn't often home for dinner. Augusta had been the daughter who took on the care of her mother when she realized the extent of her illness. She and Gertrud were close but as the eldest, Augusta felt the obligation more. Her son was moving along at Walnut Hills. She and her mother had planned his future with care. It was on schedule. Aside from attending school and sporting events, Augusta had little to do with Charles at this time. She would be called "grieving" but she was really enjoying a chance to plan a different life than she previously lived. Louisa came to her and took her hand.

"Please, Augusta, come join Elise and I in our outreach program. We need someone with contacts who can help us ensure Ohio is one of the first States to ratify the 19th Amendment." As insurance, Louisa added, "Your mother and Frank would be so proud of you."

Gertrud was the mother of three small girls. She had spent the last week of her own mothers' life sorting out clothing and accessories for the beginning of school. The youngest would be in pre-school and Gertrud would then be free to sort out hair grips and slides, ribbons and stockings. The last years had been hectic and John was not engaged in the girls' activities, dreams, or aspirations. He preferred to attend sporting events with Charles.

Most of the family had received some kind of marching orders before Eva was cold in her grave. It was effective and efficient. Eva would truly have clapped her hands to let Frank know of her approval.

After the meeting, Emilia, William and Herman found Elise and they went back to the Clifton Avenue house. It was clear that William needed more monitoring. Elise was close enough to help Emilia with basic care when needed. Greta and Angelika had moved back and now ran the house. And Herman? Elise looked at him thoughtfully.

"Herman, what do we need to keep this household running smoothly?" If he can put it into words it may make sense decided Elise.

"I thought you would never ask, Elise. It is running smoothly enough although you can see the toll it is taking on our mother. She truly loved William and was the very last to admit his mind was no longer reliable. I have watched her and fear she will also give up if she does not have a break in her current routine. We need a night nurse at the very least."

"Done!" Elise knew Frank would be happy to see this happen. He would have no regrets if his wife and her mother were happy and he did not have to commit his own time. When Eva's Estate was settled, money would not be a concern.

"Herman, there is something else I want to ask you. You seem happy and almost back to your old self again, even with the burden of an aging father and an exhausted mother to keep you engaged. But you too have a life and I want to know what you see ahead for Herman Holtz." Elise hadn't been sure she could make this speech. Confrontations had been few of late and she was out of practice.

There was a pause and both looked out the window, as if seeking a clue to the future. Finally, Herman spoke. "Elise, I have been useless, hopeless, and sick for some months. More than I want to count. But before the accident and my good luck in surviving it, I was at a high point in my life. Not being in the German Army, believe me, that was truly a nightmare, except for my partner, rest his soul. I love aviation. I love to fly. I believe it is the future. How can I convince Frank that I need to have some say in the business?"

Elise was astounded. She thought Herman might want to marry. She had seen him with Angelika and liked them as a couple. He had leaped past her modest expectations.

"Well, Herman, I suggest you draft a paper with your

rationale, your vision, and your possible part in changing the direction of the company. Frank always does better with something he can read more than once. I will help you if I can."

Herman smiled. He felt he was back in the nursery again with Elise telling him what to do and how to do it. He had already started writing but kept that part of his plans to share later with the Board, not with Frank alone.

Chapter 16

Herman's Plan

Before 1916, Die Fliegertruppen des Deutchen Kaiserreiches had been formed in Germany. By 1918 there were 2,709 front-line aircraft, 56 airships, and 186 balloon detachments used for artillery spotting. And new types of aircraft were under development. All of Europe seemed completely involved in the production of things that flew.

Vickers, in England, was producing machine guns by 1912. And France was at the forefront in experimentation. Wilbur Wright had toured France and secured a French manufacturer to produce planes designed in Ohio.

Early in 1915, Roland Garros, a French ace, had been captured with one experimental plane. It was taken to the Fokker factory and they were able to synchronize the machine gun and the propellers of planes. Formerly, pilots had shot handguns while leaning out of the window of the plane, not the best use of their skills. The lessons learned from the French plane led to the production of the Fokker Eindecker, a single seat plane, sent out in pairs to strafe trenches or to fly reconnaissance missions. Herman flew as a spotter in the first units aloft, using a two-seater plane assigned to a specific unit on the ground. His career ended when his plane crashed and burned in the battle of Verdun.

In the years before the war, little was happening in the field of flight in America. While the Wright Brothers were national heroes, the U. S. Department of War showed little interest in combat planes, considering cavalry the mobile portion of war. Luckily, other private businesses and corporations were working to develop commercial planes and Ohio was becoming the home of innovations in aviation. Cleveland and Akron were the centers for this effort.

Herman searched out information about the state of aviation in America over the past month. He knew only a little, but it was enough to realize that the country was far behind Europe and Russia. At this time, France and Britain were rebuilding their countries. It was time for America to honor the Wright Brothers and take the lead in the sky once again.

Herman's ally in getting information was Louis, Frank and Elise's chauffeur, who had driven Elise on the journey to the hospital in Canada where they found him. He and Louis were the closest of friends because of their interest in machines that move on land, sea or in the air. F & B Industries had moved from armaments to household products after the Civil War, a decision William Holtz enthusiastically participated in accomplishing. And then WWI changed the focus once again. Herman knew that this was not the time to go back to vacuum cleaners and refrigeration. He hoped to bring his brief experience in Germany to the benefit of America.

He and Louis planned to take a road trip. The scheduled stops were Akron, Cleveland, and Dayton: all in Ohio and easily reached. Herman asked for interviews with several companies and also requested a tour of The Wright Aeronautical Laboratory, not yet fully functioning but with great promise for research. Despite their hesitation, the Department of War had contracted with the Wright's Company to design a military airplane. Making plans was easy. Herman knew how much he was needed at home. He talked to the women who would have to provide support for his parents before he approached Frank. First Elise.

On her next visit, Herman caught Elise before she left the house. "We need to talk, Elise, I have a plan but will abide by your decision. It is important, but it can wait if you feel it necessary. I would be gone for about two weeks."

Elise sat down on the nearest chair. She hadn't gotten used to Herman being well and active. This was a surprise. Frank would leave in a few days, Willie had not yet returned, William and Emilia were a constant worry. Herman had been her ace in the hole. How could he leave? "Why must you leave? Where are you going?" Surely not another bolt for Washington!

Herman told her of his visits and appointments. This news was a relief. To lose all the men in her life to the Capitol was asking too much. Herman would be in Ohio, a much better location. "I will help you make this happen.

We need more help and I do know where I can find it. My contacts through our Women's Committees seem to assist as many men as women and I hope you remember this when you vote, Herman." Elise was only half joking. And now she would explain to Frank what they had decided. It would not affect him and so no problem was expected.

Herman and Elise found Greta and Angelika with William. They were preparing him for the day ahead and all was well. Emilia had taken this time to visit the hospital where she was still involved and welcome. After Herman and Elise told William's caregivers what was planned, Greta asked only one thing. "We need more household help. Perhaps a part-time cleaning lady, perhaps add more hours for the cook. We can do this."

By the time Emilia returned, the trip was settled, Elise was searching her contact list for names, and Herman had gone looking for Louis. They left the day after Frank got on a train east.

The trip was very different than their last. Herman not only spoke, he was able to drive. Cincinnati was a mecca for culture: symphony, museums, theaters, and parks. Cincinnati had all the trappings of the good life and a great number of diverse businesses that provided employment. But Cleveland and Akron held the center of all things related to aviation. The early development of planes for commercial use was found in these two Ohio cities. Before WWI, a business dedicated to steel products transferred their focus from automobiles to aircraft. They created an environment attracting talented aviation pioneers from all over the country. Glenn Martin, designer of the first aluminum skinned combat plane, was one. The company, SIFCO, was thriving. This was the first stop for the two travelers.

After being a student for the greater part of his life, Herman found he had a lot to offer. His early attachment to his father's mechanical problems gave him a background in the process of finding solutions to simple inventions. This was supplemented by the extra courses he and Willie had taken at the Technical Institute in Cincinnati, an addition to their regular academic high school program. And then, his training in Germany, almost submerged in theory, application, and action for over a year. He grew up and treasured all he learned. His mind went through procedures many times: it was his hold on sanity while he recuperated after the crash.

At his first meetings with engineers at SIFCO and Goodyear, he was amazed at the warm reception from those working to develop new concepts he had already seen in progress. It was difficult to leave for Dayton and even harder to leave for home. Both men returned with a strong desire to leave again as soon as possible.

The changes in the family were easy to see in as little as two weeks. Gertrud and John Alden, with their three daughters, moved into Eva's home in Avondale. For now, their small house in Clifton would remain vacant. Augusta and Roger created a study for the new manager of F & B both at home and at the factory. And as Emilia and William's household grew, Elise found it working well. She had more free time for her own special projects once again.

One change did catch the attention of family but no one cared to discuss it at length. In the end, Louisa moved into the Clifton house with Elise and the children. There were no arguments posed by any family member.

Chapter 17

The Women Meet

"**E**lise, catch your breath. Good. We are in a brief moment of calm before your children come home. Augusta is ready to engage with us. Your Mama wans to engage with us. And before another large community meeting, we need to sort out our agenda." Louisa spoke firmly, sure the time was right.

"Absolutely, my dear friend. I have already asked Augusta for next Tuesday and I will pick up Mama early enough so she cannot disappear. She had missed the hospital but could use more than one escape from the sick room." Elise smiled at her friend and they shook hands as they used to do in school.

Tuesday came in its usual order. It is not easy to get even a small group of women together on a weekday, there are routines built into their calendar. And if there are not, it is not good to let others believe you are free whenever they call.

Louisa began the small group discussion to set reasonable boundaries to their talk. "I am going to assume that women will be voting in the 1920 Election. If they don't it will be because we haven't gotten the message out, not because it isn't legal. Now, this is fine but none have handled a ballot before, and none have decided on the issues that will probably be on that ballot. And so we have a bigger job. Getting out the vote is only as meaningful as the mind that checks the ballot."

"But Louisa, we do not have a ballot! We don't know what will be on the ballot we do not have. How will you inform them without any idea?" Augusta was disgusted already.

"Actually, Augusta, we can read the newspapers, listen to the radio, and attend the many debates and speeches that will soon begin." Louisa said this pleasantly enough but Augusta was considering leaving the vote up to the men, as it had always been done.

Emilia spoke at just the right time. "Ladies, we have an obligation to the future. Men have not done so well with their vote that we can leave the totality of the future in their hands. Augusta, would you like Charles to set your course when he is of age and you are l an old woman?"

"Of course you are right, Emilia. But then, let us discuss now, before there are dozens voicing their opinions at once. What are the issues?" Augusta was digesting the old woman remark. Was it an omen or just badly delivered?

"I propose that in the next few weeks we each, with some research into current news, present a possible issue that will determine which candidate will be chosen to represent Democrats or Republicans. And we endorse neither party!" Louisa had told Elise of this proposal and asked her, as an example, to offer an issue of concern.

Elise felt brave enough to bring up the issue of Black Americans. "Slavery is ended, Black Americans served in the U.S. Army yet they are treated badly. They wish to join Unions but are not welcomed, they earn enough to buy houses but they are not encouraged to do so or they must buy in areas designated by the city or town. In some areas, churches attended by black citizens have been burned. And there have been both lynchings and riots. We need a candidate for President who will address this and actively work to stop the illegal acts against the black citizens of our country."

Emilia clapped. Louisa said, "Hear, hear, Elise." And Augusta quietly left the room. This did appear to be duty calling and not a reaction to Elise and so the group disbanded. Emilia, Elise and Louisa sat alone and silent for a few minutes.

"This will be a case of being wrong whatever path you take, Elise. You could have called for open zoning or the end of prohibition. We need votes and not every woman will agree with your concerns. So what do you do? I think this was a good moment. And now decide. Do you want the vote for women? If you say yes you have to allow that not all the votes you get will reflect the choices you want. You are in a democracy and so it must be." Emilia patted Elise as if she were a small girl who had just ruined her best dress by climbing a tree. "Be brave again and your vote will count. Some day you will be on the ballot and your fight will not be yours alone."

They decided not to use race as an example. "And so," Louise laughed, "We can choose an issue that will be equally divisive. Universal health cares anyone? Family Planning clinics?"

"I think I will choose the League of Nations. There will be those for and against but it is a little less close to home."

When they left Elise's comfortable breakfast room, they were happy because the meeting was over. It needed to happen and they learned something that would be helpful. It was decided that Louisa would make contact with Augusta and explain their decision. The next concern would be global rather than local.

Elise depended on Willie for talking through problems in her life. His absence was unfortunate. However, Frank would be back in D.C. soon and then Willie could come home. His grasp on economic matters would be a tremendous help in determining the next presentations. So many families, some without a husband or father, were living in poverty. Elise was entering into the doors of the black community more and more often. She saw the suffering and noted that some of the single mothers were the wives of veterans who did not return from war. They needed help.

Elise was worried about the election. In her heart she knew that women would be voting. Then she sat up and recovered her poise. "When Willie returns, Louisa and I will find a time when he can direct us towards a source of information not completely tied to a party point of view. Although that might not be as bad as it sounds. People need to know what the party they choose stands for in an election." She was done for the day. The children were home and she could hear them calling her from the floor below.

"Thank God they can't vote." This was Elise's last comment as she walked back downstairs.

Chapter 18

Opportunity Knocks

Frank arrived in Washington energized and ready for anything at all that was unrelated to family matters. It was dark and late. He felt the vibrations of the city entering every pore. He had alerted Willie and his room was ready. Willie had booked into a small hotel in preparation for leaving within a few days.

Early the next morning, Frank reported to his colleague, supervisor, or, to be more honest, his boss. The boss was not an elected official. He was, in part, civil service and, in part, a contracted analyst. That is, he analyzed what his boss wanted him to do and made it happen. He and Frank got along well and both were determined to survive the next election and remain in D.C.

They were glad to see each other again for very different reasons. Frank asked, "How did my brother-in-law do while I was gone? Did he manage to hide his own opinions when it was important for him to look neutral?"

"He did. He was invaluable."

Frank was not too pleased to hear this. "In what area

did he meet your needs? I do believe you worked with a true Wilson advocate this last week."

The boss replied with a smile. "It doesn't matter, Frank. I have a new charge. I will be going to Brussels very soon for preparatory meetings of the ILO to be held there next year. Chances are good that our point of view will be more acceptable by then. I have put in a request for you to accompany me as one with multiple contacts in the countries involved in the talks. And as a businessman who has hired and fired workers in his past life."

Frank got a grip. He had been surprised, then depressed, and now elated. If he could hang in until after the election there might still be a chance that he could avoid resettling in Ohio. He would have to wait and see. "What an opportunity! I am grateful that you chose me instead of Willie."

Willie was younger, had academic credentials and a pleasant non-confrontational way of stating his views. On the other hand, Willie had a metal contraption in place of a leg. That would surely take away some of his better points. Frank believed in physical fitness at any age.

However, as the "boss" pointed out, "Willie's politics are on the ascendant today. That will not last long, I predict a great change in less than a year."

Willie had not been told the second part of this saga. If the boss and Frank were to go to Belgium, then Willie would pick up the job they were leaving behind. Everyone liked Willie and respected his competence. It was a win/win situation. If Willie chose to do it, he could keep Frank's room warm and his information fresh.

Frank found out that night. Although not officially told, Willie had heard enough to realize he was being considered for the job Frank was abandoning for the moment. Willie was delighted. He felt strongly about the economic forecast he was preparing to present for the team's approval. He was reasonably sure they would not approve it. If he stayed on and could demonstrate its validity, it might just influence the direction of the next four or more years.

It was easy to see that, both Frank and Willie were dedicated to assisting their country and willing to ask family and friends to accept their absence on those grounds. The two talked about changes at home and possible scenarios into the wee hours of the night. It had been two nights without sleep for Frank and he felt marvelous. While Frank began to pack to leave the Georgetown room tidy for Willie, he was sure he would return to it soon. Willie would not survive the election and the change of direction Frank forecast.

Willie was in his element as well. Since his down time recovering and adjusting to the loss of his leg, he had become a devoted reader. Elise helped in this effort. It was his sister, once again, who pushed him to become acquainted with both English and German classics. When he was accepted at the University of Cincinnati, his major was a toss up. Willie started as a German major, switched to history and found himself in graduate school as a political science major focused on economics. International politics took him forward towards his advanced degree as an Honors Scholar. It was almost accomplished and he was classified as and ABD = all but thesis acceptance and degree. This job would provide that piece of writing and he was drafting it in his had already.

How does a national election influence the course of International affairs? He would create two distinct pathways and see which was chosen. And, also, how it worked out for the country and the global economy. The position of civil servant qualified as the required "experience" and in a year he might very well be Professor William Holtz. His father would be proud, if he remembered who Willie was.

Neither of the two men, separated by age and up-bringing but confident and ambitious in their current lives, had talked about the far reach of their decisions. Frank knew Elise could cope without him. Willie was less sure about Louisa but again; he depended on Elise to take care of the home front. First thing, next morning, he would call Elise. No, he would call Louisa. He finally decided to sleep on the decision.

Before sleep came, Willie remembered that he had a message for Frank from a young woman who had come to visit him at his room. He explained that he was Frank's wife's brother and that Frank would return soon. She had seemed upset at that point and only said, "No message until he is back."

Chapter 19

At Home in Ohio

The call came through about 10:00 in the morning. The children were at school and Elise had a few minutes to think over what Willie had told her. No word from Frank as yet. And she didn't know if Louisa had been notified first. "Oh Willie." Elise saw the small brother he had been when she closed her eyes. In some ways, even if he were a Professor, he would always be the same. And she would always be there for him. When Elise thought of family in the privacy of her mind, the images flashing before her were Emilia, Willie, and Herman. If she forced the issue, William Frederick, Eva Emilia and Max emerged, then Eva and Louisa and finally Frank. It was a hierarchy established over time and practice. The changes made by Eva's passing were extensive. Her death had certainly altered Frank's connection to Cincinnati: it was non-existent.

Regardless of the events at the nation's capitol, there were things to do at home. A general meeting of the new League of Women Voters for Cincinnati and Hamilton County would be held next week to determine the issues to be stressed before the election. The National League of Women Voters was formally in place to unite all existing organizations. The overarching vision must be understood before the election. And no longer was the vote restricted to the Alpha Male. The Queen Bees would make their appearance at the ballot box.

Elise and Louisa were delighted with the League's philosophy. Its focus on study and action leading to consensus among all was a mantra they could support. Materials, resources, technical experts and public officials lent substance to their final goals. The two women started their hand-out with a listing of League beliefs: respect for individuals, the value of diversity, inclusion of grassroots input, and the power of collective decision making.

The program adopted in 1920 had 69 considered issues. Briefly, they included child welfare, education, home financial health, women on the work force, public health, and independent citizenship for married women. Each of these headings contained a list of relevant subjects.

Elise read it with some doubt. She had adopted the black community as part of her own grassroots group and wanted to see them specifically named as participants. It might be considered under the part about respect for the individual but she doubted that. There was also a significant lack of concern for immigrants. "Next time," Elise vowed to Louisa.

In truth, Louisa had noted a significant distancing of the white ladies from the small number of black women who attended the meetings. "Of course, Elise, all of these issues will be addressed as the League grows stronger. The important thing is that some are here in the hall with us. They will not be strangers forever."

That did not end the conversation. Elise continued, "Fair labor laws for women and the same wage for the same work would be a helpful start. Also, labor laws protecting children need to be brought to the forefront. If these issues are not addressed by the League, who will put them on the table?"

"I see your point but I am more concerned that the League does not become so divided that it accomplishes nothing. Can't you see a group of men laughing at the picture of women fighting with each other over these concerns? I can." Louisa stopped to catch her breath. As yet, she had not told Elise that her certification to teach had come through. She intended to enter the work force as soon as a job opening appeared. And she was not interested in teaching the children of the rich. Louisa would meet her own goals in her own way, independent of the League or anyone else.

The small diversion was not unusual for Elise and Louisa. They depended on these arguments to improve the ability to express their feelings. Frank had no idea what was really going through his wife's imaginings. Willie did know of Louisa's ambitions and applauded them whenever possible.

The meeting in the community hall was well attended and the League's list accepted by consensus. It would now be up to the group to divide into committees, execute a task, and ensure women really did reach the ballot box.

And so they did. It was clear after the election that

women did not vote as a bloc. The new President, Warren G. Harding, was a former State Senator in Ohio, the Governor of Ohio, and Ohio's choice for the Senate of the United States. His candidacy was most informal: there was no touring across the country, no huge rallies at distant cities. He stayed pretty much on his own front porch. And he was from Ohio. "Normalcy" was the keynote. No more wars.

The first President to enter office with the support of many women had a few flaws. His Cabinet and administrative offices were filled with friends and people he could trust. Unfortunately this was a mistake as his friends in high places used their positions to fill their pockets. The Teapot Dome scandal was one of many during Harding's brief time in office. He died before the end of his first term, putting Vice President Calvin Coolidge in the Oval Office. Harding was a friendly, affable man, perhaps too much so with the ladies. His early death did elicit some rumors but in all, the country let him rest in peace.

And the League was up and running, ready for the challenge of a new election. The process was in place. Now the non-partisan pledge of the League would be truly tested.

It almost seemed as though Elise and Louisa were testing themselves. At the close of the meeting the two left the hall and walked back to the Clifton Avenue house. The dining room table was strewn with paper and teacups so they retreated to the breakfast room behind it. This room had abundant sunlight, streaming in from a large bay window. A seat had been built into the sill and there they sat, pleased with everything that was happening.

"I have an idea you may like, Louisa. Please tell me exactly what you think, no fudging the problems involved. I think you should move into this house to be with me and the children. Break your lease or buy out the contract and move soon. It will save money, it will help with the children and I would be delighted to argue with you whenever possible."

Chapter 20

A Career Unravels

During his short time in office, Warren Harding set a standard in Washington that was very much in tune with the jazz age. Morality was not a dominant feature in any sense, fiscal or otherwise. This affected Frank directly. A strong mother governed his actions before he could walk alone. Her influence was directed at behaviors that could affect his standing in society. Eva's goals for her son did not include his personal and private behavior. That alone ensured his loyalty. Unfortunately, this lack of oversight had much to do with Frank's character as an adult.

When he left Washington as one of America's representatives to the coming Brussels conference, he left his mark behind him. One of the young secretaries in the office had fallen in love with Frank. His charm worked well on a young girl on her own for the first time in a city she considered magic. Most of Frank's nights on the town included Annie Tolson. They were a couple in the sense of the times. Away from home, gentlemen often created a new persona that included a partner. At least that was Frank's observation.

Frank did take the time to explain his trip to Europe before leaving. Annie was assured that he would return. He explained that his brother, Willie, would occupy "their room". He decided not to explain that Willie was his wife's brother, not his own. Neither Annie nor Frank knew at the time that she was pregnant.

In the excitement of the move, Annie was more or less ignored. She understood and was sure that they would communicate freely once Frank had a new address to share. At the office, things continued to function. Willie joined the crew and was accepted as Frank's temporary replacement. All was well until Annie found out that Willie was Frank's brother-in-law and that home in Cincinnati, Frank had a wife and three children.

No one was aware of the unfolding drama. Papers were typed, more scribbles were produced for typing, reports were dictated and typed as well. No change in routine meant all would continue as it had before Frank had joined the crew. Except for the coming baby. Annie realized that her only chance was to have Frank divorce his wife and marry her quickly. It didn't take long for her to realize that this would not happen. Willie described his sister and the children well enough for Annie to understand the permanency of the marriage. Her options were few.

A month after Frank left, Annie Tolson visited an illegal abortion provider. She had managed to get home after the procedure and bled to death during that night.

When she did not appear at work the next day it was not a problem, but the following day another friend from the office went to her rooms to check. She was told that the ambulance had taken Annie the morning before and they were waiting to hear from her family about the disposition of her remains.

The sad news quickly made the rounds in Frank's office and in others. It was not the first time but it was so badly managed that a response was necessary. Frank was let go, with regrets but with firm orders to return to Washington to sign out and pack once again for Ohio.

Within a short time, Frank found himself no longer his mother's pride and joy, no longer the lover of a beautiful young woman, and no longer employed by the civil service. It shocked him badly. He easily excused himself.

"If Annie had told me I could have made it right." This comforted Frank so he said it often. His supervisor was notified and assured Frank that although he had to go back to Washington, he would soon blow over and he would be restored. Both Frank and his boss knew that the end of the Harding administration would mark the end of life as they had known it. Coolidge had promised to clean house and Frank might well be the first to be swept away.

Frank had no idea if Elise knew. He was sure Willie would not tell her. Maybe. The trip to Belgium by ship had been another lark. The trip back would not be. And when he did enter his old room, would Willie still be there, waiting to see whether the place was his for the long term? While thinking these thoughts Frank was packing.

He had shared a hotel room with his boss who had kindly left him on his own for the day.

By late afternoon, Frank packed and made a decision. He was on a train to Berlin where he could tell family in Ohio he was going to look for those relatives still in residence. Where he did not know.

Berlin looked different. The damage to the city was not as bad as he had heard. Paris and London had suffered more. In very little time Frank found that the city was very much alive. Creativity had come with the Weimar Republic and from the Bauhaus movement through architecture, music and film Berlin held all he could ask for. The nightlife roared louder than Washington's and the crime that was evident was only a small drawback. Prostitution, drug and alcohol abuse, theft and murder were all present however. The upper and rising middle class moved above those impediments to total enjoyment of the moment.

Frank made another decision. He would find work. Perhaps at one of the organizations formed to integrate Germany with Europe once again. A Conference was slated for Locarno in the not too distant future. His past credentials might get him a seat at that event. He would surely try, even if he could not locate family to help him. The picture Elise had painted of Germany could not have been further from the reality.

As he walked down the Unter den Linden on a fine Sunday afternoon, Frank saw a familiar face. Eva had a new maid a few years back, hired by his mother to watch Elise during her visit to Germany and to report back.

The Melting Pot: 1919-1939

Sonia had come to Ohio from Paris and needed a position. Her family had been highly placed in the government of France at one time and made poor political choices while in office. Sonia had asked her brother to help her leave France for America to avoid incarceration. Frank sympathized with that and encouraged his mother to hire the new arrival.

The past skipped through his memory and he saw his luck change. He called out, "Miss! Please wait!" in English and she stopped and turned to him.

"Sonia! Whatever are you doing here? Does Louis know where you are?" The meeting astonished Frank. He knew Sonia had married and stayed in Germany when Elise left some years ago. He did not know that Sonia and Louis, the family chauffeur stayed in touch. He soon found out that Sonia's husband died in the war, she had a daughter six years old, and a lack of money to live on. Her husband had left her fairly well off but inflation had decimated her savings and the future was not bright.

As they talked, Frank found Sonia the repository of all his German family information. The start of his new life began with that meeting. He had a way to contact the few family members still alive and living in Berlin. In return, Frank promised to find a way to return Sonia to Cincinnati.

Chapter 21

The Children Adjust to a New Normal

Mama had received a letter from abroad. William Frederick watched the envelope closely, waiting for an opportunity to take possession of the stamps. Eva Emilia looked at her mother's face to determine if the news were good. Max sat in a corner vacillating between anger and tears. He had another encounter with Aunt Louisa that turned out badly for him.

They sat together in the breakfast room, which was really the center of family activities. They ate breakfast there in stages, depending on their schedule. They also ate lunch and dinner there since Frank left. It was a large room at the back of the house. A separate much smaller room adjoined it. This was the pantry, service area, and the dumbwaiter space. It accommodated snacks and received all entrees from the kitchen, located a floor below. In past years, Frederick and Eva E. had enjoyed placing Max in the dumbwaiter and lowering him to the kitchen. One day they were diverted by a sudden visitor and forgot their original activity. Max's yells finally caught the attention of Louis who was washing the car outside the kitchen door. It was the last ride for Max.

One corner of the room held a large fireplace, big enough to sit in when not in use. The room's large table, small sofa and easy chairs combined to provide comfort and less formal behavior. Aside from the nursery, it was the children's favorite room in the house proper. All three would have chosen to live in the carriage house with Louis if allowed.

Louisa was a tyrant in the other downstairs rooms. This was acceptable to his siblings but not to Max. His thoughts on Louisa were directly opposite theirs. Max was concentrating on what should happen to his aunt and finally asked, "When is father coming home?" This would end the current situation, remove Aunt Louisa, and bring a sense of normalcy back to the family.

Elise laughed. "It is amazing you should ask, Max. This is a letter from your father. He is in Germany and he has found Sonia!"

None of the children knew Sonia. They had heard Louis, the family driver, speak about her to Elise from time to time but it made no sense. Why would his sister live in Germany? They were from France. Louis told them this constantly. Why would their father meet Sonia in Germany, and was this the reason he was not on his way home? The questions continued to fill the room with interest and some anxiety. Elise was at a loss.

"Read us the letter, Elise. Some parts of it need to be heard. It would inform us all at the same time, that was one of Frank's special concerns." Louisa sat patiently and heard in Frank's own words of his meeting with Sonia, his continued search for lost relatives and the possibility of bringing Sonia and her daughter to America. He forgot to send greetings to his children but Elise thoughtfully added that message. It was not the letter that Elise expected but it was not a surprise. His return to Cincinnati seemed far in the future and she was relieved to hear confirmation of his continued absence.

"Change your clothes, children! You still have an hour or so to enjoy being outside." Elise was eager to talk over the next steps with Louisa. The path ahead was clear of one obstacle.

William Frederick eyed the envelope before rushing out of the room. Louisa noticed this and carefully passed it to him as he reached the door. It was a small enough token from his father after months of absence. When Willie next came home, Louisa would be sure to have him talk about the work he and Frank were doing for the country. She would like to know that too so Willie would have a large audience. It was Frederick who concerned both women the most. He had counted on his father's advice after entering Walnut Hills. One grand mama was now gone. That left one who knew nothing about his school. His aunts, Augusta and Gertrud had different opinions. Cousin Charles got on the same bus as he did and seemed pleased with his assignments and classes. Aunt Gertrud's three daughters were younger but Frederick had a feeling that they would not get on the bus with their cousins in the next few years. He had tested well enough to enter Walnut Hills. Perhaps Eva Emilia would not.

William Frederick was out of touch with his family. Elise had decided when Eva Emilia was born that her daughter would have the same education as her older brother. At this time, Elise was researching tutors to ensure her daughter's acceptance into the College Prep High School with the best reputation. If that failed, she would explore St. Xavier. After all, the family had been Catholic until she married and changed her denomination to suit Frank's family.

Eva Emilia had some thoughts of her own. Free time was short since her school schedule no longer fit with William Frederick's. He was also involved in sports after classes and that brought him home later and later. She very much wanted her brother to enchant her with the beauties and benefits of Walnut Hills. Both Eva E. as was called, and Rick, as he was nicknamed, were interested in nature and when much younger, they would spend a great deal of time in the forest behind the house.

Through Emilia, Eva E. had a large interest in nursing and health. Emilia had taken her to visit the hospital not long ago. It especially appealed to Eva E. who thought well of Emilia as a grandmother Emilia was gratified by her attention and noted that nursing had a much better reputation in Ohio than it had in Germany.

Max was a surprise to his parents and his siblings. He had possibilities but they were obscured by his violent response to anything that displeased him. This characteristic Elise attributed to his Grand Mama Eva.

His favorite activity was sport. Any sport, but soccer preferred. His father had begun to include him at baseball games but Max would rather kick a ball than hit it with a stick. He was a nosy little boy, interested in what was happening around him, even if it wasn't his business. People learned to guard their tongues when Max was in the room.

"Well, they are very different children. Three with the same disposition and energy would be daunting." There were other high schools in the city. East Side, Hughes and Woodward were close. One goal Elise kept even from Louisa. Her children would understand and speak German. Heritage had its good points and the connection to the past was one. Their grandparents and great-grandparents had chosen to come to America, but not as blank slates. They brought cultural embellishments that only made America greater. The idea was to choose the very best of what you are offered.

Meanwhile, Louisa settled in. The bedroom that had been Elise and Frank's sanctuary now sheltered Elise and Louisa. A new kind of family was formed.

Chapter 22

America Expands

President Harding was the first of a long period of Republican Presidents. When he unexpectedly died while on a trip in 1923, he was succeeded by Vice= President Coolidge. Silent Cal was ready to clean house but he had little interest in domestic reform or International politics. Rural America was ready for normalcy, the cities were alive with radio, movies, jazz, bootleg liquor and flappers. Advertising became a business. The Mafia thrived and expanded, defying the law and the Untouchables, at least until a strategy was in place that worked.

And new arrivals added to the population. The census reported that between 1880 and 1920, four million Italians and two million Jews had come to America. And then came the flurry of laws to regulate just who was welcome. The Chinese Exclusion Act was the first to specify a group. An 1891 Immigration Act barred polygamists, criminals, the sick and diseased. The Federal Office of Immigration opened Ellis Island and between 1892-1954 1.2 million new arrivals entered through this door.

The question of an open door remained open. The

Jean Romano

Immigration Act of 1924 set quotas by nationality. Great Britain, Ireland and Germany composed 70% of all allowed by law, however, illegal entry increased, most especially from Asia.

Into this on-going legal confusion came the problem of Sonia. She had been true to Elise and Elise was about to return the favor. She enlisted Louis as a citizen and family member to sponsor his sister. Elise would promise her a job.

The position Elise had in mind would depend on a number of things. The children were growing quickly but could still use tutorial help with languages. Sonia would fit that need. Or, William and Emilia both needed more help although for different reasons. Emilia was so restricted by her duties as caregiver that her own health was jeopardized. William lapsed further into his own imaginings and had little connection to the present moment. He would have to be watched at all times.

As family members spread out across the globe once again, adjustments were in order. After Frank left, Louisa had become the daily confidant of her sister-in-law, and when Willie went to visit Frank, their friendship grew. It was a rare day that didn't start with a call from one to the other. No major decisions were made without consultation. This stopped and left a vacuum in all their relationships after Frank decided to remain in Germany.

Elise and Louisa retreated to the master bedroom for a moment of sharing. They would sort out the family as it was now. The door was closed. The huge four-poster stood at one end of the room and at the other was the massive Rookwood fireplace. The two women sat in the chairs facing the fireplace as Elise and Frank had in the past.

Elise started the conversation with the basics. "We have income, but it is limited to what Frank has set up with his brother-in-law, based on Eva's estate. I can't count on it and see no way to discuss this with either Frank or his lawyer."

"An issue to be sure. As I remember terms of the Will, Eva recognized that Frank needed a steady hand on his inheritance and I recall that you are joint inheritors. I do believe Eva worried about her grandchildren even more than she did her son." Louisa was mentally counting credits and debits. "And, Elise, I am now officially teaching in the Cincinnati Public Schools. That is guaranteed and the salary is in my name only!"

Elise had her initial speech ready. "If we want to be certain of meeting our needs, let's count only what we are sure of until we can talk to Willie. As it is, Emilia and William can afford to maintain their home and pay Greta and Angelika to help. They seem able to afford a cook and cleaning help as well. We will make their transportation needs available through Louis." Elise had discussed this with Emilia and felt reassured about some of the family under her protection. "And, Louisa, there is Herman in that household, ready and able to work. He wants to work! He told me so just last week."

"That leaves Frank's sisters and their family. Both of the husbands are now employed by F & B Industries and it appears they like being in charge of something. I think

Eva discouraged them before now, she had definite views on every phase of the business." Louisa was amazed at the control Eva had exerted on behalf of the family. And Eva's Will clearly showed far reaching plans for the next generation of Freimarcks.

"Here again, we need Willie to sort out the distribution of profits. Louisa, has Willie mentioned a trip home in the near future?" Elise had been asking this question for some time. This day brought welcome news. Willie would be coming home in two weeks for a short visit to pack what he needed and to help his wife and sister plan the family budget.

'Willie says the economy is doing well and the business is thriving. The change of focus he prescribed was the correct answer to a post-war economy. We are providing what is needed abroad and all of our industries are offering jobs that enrich the lower classes. I personally hate the sound of that, but full employment is good for the country as a whole." Louisa was never quite sure what social class embraced her. Her reputation as the child of a divorced mother followed her like an invisible cloud throughout her life.

Nothing could be settled until Willie advised them further but it seemed that for the moment, barring any extraordinary news from Frank, all would be manageable.

"There is just one problem left, Louisa. We must reconfigure our sleeping arrangements while Willie is here."

Chapter 23

The Man of the Times

Willie saw Louis waving at the end of the station house. This was not the same place where his accident cost him a leg. Willie could enjoy the return without memories that could stay unopened. On the ride home, Louis explained Sonia's predicament and asked advice. Willie gave him the names of the State congressmen and suggested he begin by contacting them to find one to vouch for his stability and his sister's need. Willie did not discuss the reservations that could stop the process. The fact that Louis was asking entry for a single mother of French origin was a good start. Louis pulled into the circular driveway at the front of the house. The door opened and Elise waved him in.

They embraced then Elise stepped back to allow Louisa to give him the full welcome he deserved. All were genuinely happy to be together, despite the circumstances. Elise had combed her hair and Louisa was dressed in skirt and shirt, looking exactly as a school teacher should. "If only," thought Willie, "this was the way it appears to be." He knew better.

The breakfast room was sunny, the coffee hot, and rolls, butter and cheese provided a brief snack before dinner. Elise realized that her brother wanted to deal with their concerns before meeting the rest of the family. He understood all of the reasons for Louisa's move to the Clifton house and agreed that in matters of finance it was astute. Elise had a monthly amount paid to her own bank account through Eva's estate but little else. Willie walked her through a process guaranteed to increase that amount. If Frank did find work abroad, his share could be reassigned to his children. It began to look like their current life style would be possible. It was difficult to predict Frank's future.

Both Willie and Elise thought the other would know what Frank was planning. Frank himself didn't know. And so for now, this part was skipped. Willie encouraged Elise to stay when Roger and John, the brothers –in-law came to talk business. Louisa excused herself to return to her school for a meeting. The doorbell chimed and Willie's third conference began.

Mentally, Willie was on his game. The goal of the visit was to leave home knowing everyone knew where they stood. At the very least, there would be financial clarity. Elise had sorted out Emilia and William's needs, and with help from Herman, they seemed set.

Elise needed some financial help and this meeting should provide it. Willie intended to have Roger pay for Eva's house. Roger sold his smaller home and moved into what had been the patriarch's home. Now the bill was due. That money, invested in the company, would bring extra income to Elise. He wanted to be sure his sister was present when this deal was completed. John, the family lawyer at this point, would be charged with setting up the paper work Elise needed to be comfortable raising Frank's three children, possibly without Frank.

The talks went well. Willie was impressed with Roger's grasp of the current economy. No, the family was not the equivalent of the Carnegies, Rockefellers, or J.P. Morgan. Around that well used table, all were aware of the processes used to advance the top economic icons of their time. It was proven, in their minds, that to succeed it was necessary to assess the competition, to expand, to be big enough to produce on a scale that increased profits and absorbed competitors. Roger and John had already evaluated the situation and were ready to be absorbed, at a price, and with the added caveat that they would join the Boards of the umbrella company being formed. Willie felt his job had been reduced to child's play.

"I do have one last item on my list. This visit will be shorter than I hoped but we are making excellent progress." Willie reached into his briefcase for a yellow pad. "I can turn over a few pages! The last on my list addresses questions from both you and Louisa. Questions related to your work with Women's Suffrage. I have thought through some issues that affect women in the home, in the labor force, and in our community, which you will soon be entering officially. And any other issues you might like to discuss. Can we table this until tomorrow? My train does not leave until late afternoon."

When the breakfast room lost its guests, Willie and

Elise smiled and sighed at the same time. In some ways, this last confrontation made them feel young again. They had overcome what could have been tedious at best. Elise realized that some things should be left unsaid. She gestured to Willie's one small bag and said, "It is time to settle you in for whatever time you have here. Let's go up. You and Louisa have the boy's old bedroom. We are in the process of allowing William Frederick to have his own room but for now, Max takes up a bit of his space. Eva E. is with me and we are using our time to bond as mother and daughter. Louisa is in Eva E's old room and I think you will find it pleasant enough." This complicated game of hide and seek left Elise flustered and Willie amazed.

"You have reorganized well, Elise! I can see that the children are fast becoming adults and change is inevitable. How well you do this. One question, when will William Frederick assume a shorter name? I can tell you now that his next school will require it."

This had been a problem. William Frederick was now Rick to his friends. Elise felt it cruel to leave out the name of his grandfather, especially at this turning point in both their lives. Willie is right. There have been too many Williams and the name is not needed. "He is Rick or Fredrick from here on, Willie!"

"Good for you, and congratulations to your son. He asked for my help and for once I can fulfill a request." Willie had been dreading the issue and now that river was forded.

"And talking about rooms brings up another topic. You haven't seen the room in Washington, Elise! The nursery would be an improvement. I can't imagine living in D.C. for any great amount of time." Willie saw Elise turn white. He recovered. "I am searching for a small apartment. When Frank returns it will be a nice surprise. If our jobs over-lap there will be room for us both and all possibilities are covered. I will let Louisa know as soon as I have moved."

They continued to the second floor bedrooms. Nothing else need be said. Willie had satisfied his sister. Now it would be an extension of that feat for his wife's ear as soon as they were alone.

It did seem that all would be well on the home front. Willie looked at the bed with its frilly pink spread. Louisa was not a frilly pink person. He understood and decided that the visit would go well if some paths were unexplored. He opened his suitcase and hung up the suit he would wear at the family dinner tonight. Seeing his father would be difficult.

Then Willie opened his briefcase and laid out the papers he needed to complete before next week in Washington. His opinion had been specifically sought on issues of trade and reparations. He was not ready to hand in a blanket endorsement of any plan but he did recognize that the election had not imposed any constraints on the policies he had presented in the last weeks. The idea of raising tariffs seemed inappropriate. European countries were heavily in debt to America already. Reparations were best left to the League of Nations as the body with some method of enforcing them. And, he had noticed a different attitude towards Germany in recent days.

Despite predictions, Germany was being accepted back into the good graces of its former enemies.

Disarmament was another story. It would be more likely for weapons to be stockpiled than destroyed, except in Germany. To Willie, that determination was counterproductive. The former allies would have weapons that were obsolete while German science and technology would produce new and lethal weaponry in the event of another dispute or even another war.

Over all, what was needed was a lessening of barriers to world trade and cooperation among nations. A stable currency standard had to be in place, and some definite rules on the basis for the currency used. For Willie, gold or silver was still the answer. Paper money was easy to print but this attribute made it less valuable. How much paper would be required to pay a bill? His mind couldn't process an answer. Willie decided to sleep on this, maybe rise early and read it all again. For now, perhaps a brief nap before Louisa asked another question and it was time to dress for dinner.

There was a knock at the door.

"Willie, it's Herman. Are you awake? Do you have a moment or two before we are submerged in family? I usually plead a headache after about an hour of celebratory dinners and regardless, we would have no chance to talk. Willie, are you there?"

Willie still had his list in hand. All issues and concerns were crossed out. A little peace before the storm was all he needed. On the other hand, he loved Herman. It would be some time before another opportunity to speak to him rose and so he called, 'Come in Herman! I've been waiting for you!"

And Herman entered the room with a large manila envelope in his right hand, a pad and pencil in the other. He looked like he had as a boy, only bigger. Herman was definitely mended. Tall, dark haired, energetic and happy, Herman placed his pad on the bed and sat next to it.

Willie knew without another word that this meeting might affect all those issues he had completed satisfactorily. His brother was far too happy to be about to tell his brother that all was well and no changes would be necessary.

Chapter 24

Flight in Several Forms

A quick and manly embrace began their talk. Willie still thought of his brother as a kind of delinquent teenager, loath to take advice from anyone and full of ideas that had no basis in reality. Herman's experience in Germany had put a dent in this theory but he had rarely spoken to his brother since he returned to Cincinnati. They sat on the bed together in comfortable silence. Herman cleared his throat and it was broken.

"You can believe this, Willie, your brother Herman is asking for advice, and he is ready to consider it carefully. Don't be afraid, I haven't been drinking, it's too early for that. What I plan to do affects the family and I have caused enough trouble there to last a lifetime. So, listen and then be listened to. I will be brief." Herman adjusted his seat, pushed off a few pink pillows, and began his story.

Aviation was his love. He had suffered greatly because of it but now he was healed and ready to reenter the career he had chosen long ago. He explained to Willie the state of the art in America and how he wanted to be part of it. Herman had done his research well.

Willie looked at his brother and saw a young man with dark brown hair and mustache, many muscles, and an air of confidence that seemed to spell Airplane Pilot in smoke above his head. Herman was the Nordic male although Willie had the blond Aryan hair; Willie had never been a fan of physical fitness. Herman was always sure of foot and ready to tackle anything. At that moment Willie knew he would encourage his brother no matter how peculiar his dream was this time around. He knew that Herman should not be destined to care for aging parents: he was ready to fly.

Herman began with the Wright Brothers and Willie gently told him to move along with the story, the hour was late. Herman reddened but recognized the value of speeding up to the present. When he told Willie about the first rocket, designed by Robert Goddard, he knew he had a convert. When he skipped into the fascinating story of the Orteig Prize he lost Willie's attention for only a minute. Willie feared Herman would next say he wished to compete as the first to fly across the Atlantic. Then Willie would have to smash his dreams. Not true. Charles Lindberg was ready and his plane was being built in California by a firm owned by Benjamin Mahoney who bought it from Claude Ryan in 1925. Herman kept informed.

For a split second Willie's mind went to the phenomenon he had been watching for months: the merging of small businesses to create giant corporations centralizing the resources needed for major projects. This was an example to remember. Willie's attention came back to Herman who seemed to be describing several ventures in the field of aviation. They were located in Ohio. At last Herman got to the point that brought him to Willie's knee, so to speak. He wanted to join one of these companies. There was an opening in Cleveland and another in Dayton, a place dedicated to research. It would mean leaving Cincinnati, but he had done that before and was more than ready to do it again.

As Herman described it, Dayton was just a skip away from Cincinnati. The Dayton-Cincinnati canal connected them so effectively it was practically next-door. The important part was that Dayton was fast becoming a true center of all things related to the sky. It was the home of aeronautical and astronautical engineering and in addition to a major business investment, the U.S. Army built a base and moved many operations to the Dayton area. The Fairfield Aviation General Supply Depot was ready to offer logistics support to the Wilbur Wright Field and to Signal Corps schools for aviation. And all of these entities were expanding rapidly. There was no part of this that didn't interest Herman but the development of advanced airplane equipment and system maintenance had been one piece of his training in Germany.

Willie had a doubtful look. "Herman, your experience and training certainly give you the qualifications for a position there. It is how you became qualified that is the problem."

Herman also had doubts but convinced himself that

he could present a different picture of his earlier training. He passed muster as an American citizen. His story would be that he was conscripted while on a visit to family in Germany. It would work only if those in command felt his experience out=weighed his complete resume.

"Louis and I are planning a trip to Dayton the end of next week. I have listed my field of expertise and my hours in the air. Some of my accomplishments are left unsaid for now. If they allow me to demonstrate my skills I think it may work." Herman was no longer smiling but he had made his point.

After leaving his last family meeting Willie had decided that all was well and he could spend some time in Washington without guilt. This was a hitch in his plan. Of course, Herman should go. Life is for living. By that standard, he was also free to go.

As they parted, they wished each other good luck and vowed to keep in touch. Elise would have to pick up the pieces and her brothers were sure of her ability to do just that. Unlike their mother, Willie and Herman had never valued Elise for her beauty. There was a bit of steel in her personality that had been idle but was fully engaged now.

Herman left the room as satisfied as he had been in a long time. Willie did not rest. He dressed. The entire family, including the children's table, would be full inside the hour. Both brothers had expressed their determination to move on to work impossible in Cincinnati. It was, after all was said, the 1920's a time for experimentation for the entire world. The young should be part of that.

Chapter 25

Caregivers and the Elders

Emilia and William entered the house in dinner dress, Emilia supported by Herman and William clutching the arm of Louisa. Their son, Willie, their daughter Elise, and the in-laws still remaining in Cincinnati welcomed them. It seemed odd to Emilia that Frank was absent.

It was as pleasant a dinner party as had been arranged in many months. Willie was pleased to see how well his parents appeared. He knew that the news Herman had shared earlier would change some of their happiness. Herman had become the true caregiver but he was not well suited for the job over time. He had almost expended all the human kindness given him at birth. This made Herman feel guilty for not being more helpful and it gave Emilia a desire to see him move on to other things. She knew the psyche of caregivers personally.

Louisa was confortable with Willie's parents. Perhaps Louisa was an option? Each person present searched for an answer to the question of old age and the needs of the elderly whether they were experiencing physical or mental declines The youngest in the family were the most sympathetic but the least likely to get involved. Those already serving their elders had shifted their sympathy to themselves.

On the surface all was well. In each household there were a few problems: some were minor and some not. Emilia had been involved in the hospital for years. Now, the amount of time she could spend away from home was small, William's demands consumed her. In desperation, Emilia decided to enforce hospital standards. William was not well and if things were run with more oversight, he might recover. And so the cleaning help were monitored daily and when they did not do a job as well as she wished, Greta and Angelika were diverted from William to the chores at hand. It was a very clean house.

Herman was available for moral support whenever needed. Herman also enjoyed borrowing Elise's auto, and sometimes Louis too. He could run errands, take the family for drives and on a few occasions, leave for a short trip with Louis as guide and map-reader. Those trips were kept a secret and done under the wrap of business or auto repairs. Only Willie and Angelika knew where he went.

Herman's room was off bounds to everyone except Angelika. This romance began when he was still too ill to know who she was, and it continued to grow as he saw her attend to the needs of his parents. All had gone well until Emilia became a hospital matron rather than the wife of an elderly man who didn't know who she was. For the first time, Angelika did complain. Something had to happen. Life is not fair but it could be changed to be fairer. She had dreams of her own family and youth lasts only so long. There was proof of that under the same roof that sheltered her.

Herman and Angelika planned to marry as soon as he could support them both in whatever style they could afford. They had seen each other under the worst possible conditions but regardless of this, they wished to be enduring life together. He had not mentioned this to Willie. Emilia's harassment of Angelika was an indication that she knew. Angelika told her sister in order to cover her visits to Herman's room. It was a secret love for the moment only. Herman had described Dayton to Angelika in the most glowing terms. The Miami River sounded like the Rhine or the Danube, flowing past fields and houses to the sound of music.

Angelika was more than anxious to be there with him. And yet, Angelika had guilt wrapped around her like an old shawl. She was lost, hungry, and cold and this family had sheltered her, an immigrant from Germany, when many others were trapped in poverty. She owed them. Although she never mentioned this to Herman, Angelika vowed that she would care for his parents and siblings would always maintain a responsibility for them all. She would make up for the lapse in duty the rest of her life. And she would be the best wife in all of America.

And although Angelika was not yet included in the family dinner, she was present in Herman's heart. He was watching his brother who had not seen his parents in some weeks. In part, he forgot what was happening at home and in essence, William's decline was so steady the difference in a few days was unnoticed by those close to him.

Willie sat at the table between his father and mother. As the guest of honor, it was his right and almost the only opportunity he had to talk with them. William patted Willie's shoulder and asked, "How did you learn German?"

Willie smiled, "From you and Mama and from a tutor. The more grammatical part came from school. It was always considered important that any language be fostered and so I also studied the language at University."

"And what is your ethnicity? Were your parents German?" William asked this with an answering smile. He found this young man very charming.

Willie did not smile this time. The full import of what his father asked told him everything. William had absolutely no idea who was sitting by his side at the family dining table.

The night flew past. Emilia and William chose to leave rather early. The number of people exceeded their normal quota. Louis came to announce the car was waiting and they gracefully said their good=byes. Emilia had an extra hug for Willie, and his father said, "So glad to have met you."

After they left, there was a deep silence. Even the children were quiet for a few minutes. No words were needed.

The next morning Willie visited the University of Cincinnati to discuss his thesis with the Professor monitoring his PhD progress. The result of this meeting was positive. He was offered a position in the College of Commerce that was fairly new and in need of someone with his credentials in Political Science. As he left campus, Willie returned to thoughts of his report, due in two weeks. Washington was calling in a loud voice. It made sense now that the best report he could muster would be completed and reviewed quickly. A further assignment was probable and he would respond to any request that he could accomplish in Ohio.

The burden was lifted by the assurance of a position at the University. He would return to Cincinnati soon. It was Herman's time to fly.

The last trip Herman and Louis made to Dayton equaled Willie's success. Herman was offered a position and without consulting family, he accepted. He would be moving on to something he felt was his calling. Since Angelika had consented to marry him, he knew he would not make the next trip with only Louis. Looking into the dark eyes of Angelika, holding her willowy and graceful body, waking at night to the sound of her breath. It was a thought as enticing as flight.

Chapter 26

A Reconfiguration

The twenties continued to roar. Business was booming, larger and larger corporations emerged and exports to Europe increased. The newly formed Federal Reserve sold bonds, and American business sold stock in their companies.

By 1927, many countries returned to the Gold Standard, The New York Federal Bank loaned $150,000,000 to European Central Banks to help in their recovery. This contracted the supply of money in America because of the 40% requirement matching paper to gold. Trade went well with export and imports balanced through the foreign rate of exchange and new markets were vigorously sought in Asia.

Labor Unions formed and called strikes for better wages, hours and fairer conditions. A fear of anarchists and communists disturbed some and Unions were not without scrutiny. Nevertheless, it was a time of peace and good will, even to Germany.

The nation's population grew. The Census of 1920, the fifteenth completed in America, showed a growth of

16,253,509 people. In total, 122,275,046 Americans were noted in the official census. In 1924, the Johnson-Reed Act limited immigration to 150,000 annually. 90% of that number was allocated to those from northeastern Europe. It was also the smallest number of immigrants allowed to enter legally.

The immigrants from Germany a century ago were the largest non-English speaking group, mostly rural, and ready to set up the restaurants, guesthouses and breweries similar to those they were connected to in Germany. In 1910, there were over 500 German language newspapers and the German language was part of many school systems. In short time, these early immigrants were fully integrated but public opinion is open to change and change it did.

The opinion of the country concerning German-Americans altered during World War I. President Woodrow Wilson is quoted as follows: "Any man who carries a hyphen about with him, carries a dagger that he is ready to plunge in the vitals of this Republic when he gets ready."

German-Americans were not alone as a focus of suspicion. Although they celebrated their traditions freely until the outset of war, the teaching of German in America's schools was ended. During that same period, Russian applicants for citizenship were also a target for deportation or worse, most especially if they were suspected anarchists. The raids against Russians were part of the "Red Scare' in 1919 resulting in the round up and return to Russia of 800 considered possible anarchists or communists.

In 1917, the Espionage Act was signed into law by President Wilson and in 1918, the Sedition Act followed. Criticism of the government could mean jail or deportation. After the war as inflation rose and job loss related to the war effort increased, fear of immigrants rose. Fear is the wrong word. Americans did not cringe from the threat of immigrants. They were ready to lynch, murder, and defy justice to confront aliens who represented a different language or political philosophy.

And the federally authorized raids began. Being a member of a labor union was enough to become a target. The raids achieved little; over 80% of those arrested were released without charges and the Palmer raids stopped. As the economy improved in the '20's this practice ended but the damage was done and ignorance spawned the resurgence of the Ku Klux Klan, an organization of fear and terror that targeted Jews, Catholics and Blacks.

The Melting Pot changes its contents depending on events. Some ingredients are removed based on the easily promoted fear of the "other" identified by race, color, religion, social class, or even language.

～～

Elise looked at the paper she was preparing and sighed. "I am afraid too. I am afraid to read this to a group of women and afraid to repeat its conclusions to anyone. Louisa, Women's Suffrage is in place and I am ready for another battle. Civil Rights seem more important to me now. I read a statement by one of our national leaders, Carrie Chapman Catt, and I am astonished. She was addressing southern Senators, true, she wanted their support for the amendment, but she said clearly, 'White Supremacy will be strengthened, not weakened by women's suffrage.' Louisa, I cannot be part of a group that does not include all women."

"I know how disappointed you were by the response to the inclusion of our black neighbors at the last League meeting. Perhaps we can find common ground. Don't give up! We need to carry through on the setting of goals and the fight for registration. Virginia may plan a separate organization for black women. That may be one answer. If we don't have an immediate solution it is still better to fight from within than without!"

Elise was silent but not for long. "Surely you remember the race riots here some years back. People were burned alive in that fire. And there are signs of the Ku Klux Klan reorganizing. We cannot let this happen."

"One fight at a time, Elise! The women's vote will sort out many of the issues you want to see resolved! I am confident that this will bring about the reforms we need! In my school, I see black and white children together daily. These children will grow up without barriers. Patience and small steps are needed now." Louisa was almost breathless. She agreed with Elise but felt her sister-in-law wanted immediate results to problems that would take years to resolve.

"Louisa, there is a man who is worth following. His name is Du Bois and he is more than a match for his white detractors. He is black. In this same moment in history there is a man named Stoddard who avows that the Negro is of an inferior race. They will debate in Chicago this March. I want to be there. Would you like to join me?" Elisa had not quite decided on attending but she was caught up in an argument she felt slipping away from her.

"No Elise. But I will keep the household in order until you return." Louisa left the room. In 1929 everything looked possible and to not pursue the righteous cause would be an error. It seemed to Louisa that infringements to the rights of citizens would be solved when women added their voices to the major issues.

Louisa had clear and doable goals for the League. Elise did not. For the first time, the two parted without a hug or a smile.

Elise had made up her mind. The vote was important but even more critical was how people voted. Not Republicans, Democrats, men or women, black, white or other: what should bring Americans to the ballot box was the integrity of the country itself. The issue of black rights was her number one priority, and not just for black women. Elise told her friend that *He Passing of the Great Race* by Madison Grant would live and harm generations to come. "The rise of the Ku Klux Klan is frightening. Their attacks on blacks, Jews, and Catholics have to be recognized for the hate crimes they are. The speeches of Lothrop Stoddard reveal the ideology behind "separate but equal" for the sham it is." Elise had been affected by the anti-German actions during the war years. She identified those unjustified attacks with those on other minorities and made it her cause.

Elise did favor women's rights in every sense of the words. Men were legislating some rights specific to women on and the rights of an individual denied. Men suffered no legal consequences from an unwanted pregnancy unless they were exceptionally empathetic, women were to give birth, nurture and raise the child. This feat was to be accomplished without adequate childcare and with a lower wage than a man if the mother had to work.

Education almost replaced the first two items on her list. Federal support of public education was essential to correct the social imbalance, economic inequality, and lack of opportunity haunting the poor. An open door to the future was the right of every child.

Elise was writing her list as she thought. She had seen an article on the American Civil Liberties Union and in an attempt to communicate she found an envelope, addressed it to the ACLU and attached a stamp. It was a satisfactory conclusion to her argument with Louisa even if nothing came back in the mail. After sealing the envelope she thought of several more priorities. Elise decided to keep her list as an on-going diary of sorts, a litany of injustice that she would take as her own duty to address.

The house was quiet. Even the kitchen help had stopped their chores. It was as if the clock had stopped to reset itself, correct past time and start anew. Elise felt that the peace achieved by the war and the surge of prosperity had come in order to correct the whole of society, even the world! And that feeling of empowerment as a woman had to be gender free.

"I will try to reason with Louisa, but if she is unable to come with me, I must go down this road on my own." Elise had set a new course for herself and was ready to take the first steps alone if necessary.

Chapter 27

It's The Economy

Louis dropped Willie at the station and returned to pick up Herman for the ride to Dayton. Herman's appointment was not until tomorrow but he was determined to tour the area before his meeting with the Director.

Willie began writing on the train before Louis drove away. His pencil moved rapidly and confidently and then stopped. He looked at his numbers and decided he needed more research before committing too much to paper. The stock market was soaring, but why? It appeared strong but much of the money listed was on paper, not in the bank. The high employment and the new production of luxury goods, like automobiles, prompted a look at personal income. Willie noted that the investments in stocks were on the margin in most instances. Little cash backed up the amount of investment shown.

The urban middle class was investing through credit, through borrowing and with a new desire of the masses to become part of the elite. The elite were doing the same.

Nevertheless, only agriculture seemed to be in trouble. The report on growing surpluses rose daily.

While this wealth pursuing continued, giant corporations grew, helped by the easing of the Sherman Anti=Trust law. And they also invested. One of Willie's markers was the state of tariffs. They were low to encourage buyers. And current policy allowed the use of public and private funds to be used abroad. This would help foreign countries to buy American. Unfortunately, most of the buying was on credit. Basically, more goods were being produced than could be bought either at home or abroad.

Willie put down his pencil and hit his head with the pad. What he saw as the stars bounced off his forehead was an economy of borrowing, debt, and savings depleted or gone. Looking at past figures he also realized that as stocks went down in price, they were more attractive and more were bought: on credit, by borrowing, and with the use of savings. "Mein Gott!" Willie spoke and hit himself once more with the pad. His fellow travelers had been avoiding contact but this was the end. The conductor was asked to require better behavior from the disheveled and disabled man sitting near the back of the car.

Many countries abandoned the gold standard during the war. Britain had to impose exchange controls to keep its silver reserve. Inflation in Europe was higher than America because it remained on the gold standard and used the Federal Reserve sale of bonds to stabilize gold. In 1919 the U.S. was a creditor nation. Even though many countries returned to gold in 1927, all were affected by rising prices.

The report would wait. He would find more current information back in his office. Willie was certain he could not submit the report he had planned without committing perjury. When the trip ended and he walked into his studio room, Willie mentally kissed it good-bye. He was reasonably sure his career was going to continue at the University of Cincinnati, not Washington, D.C.

By October when the small tremors became a tidal wave of loss, Willie had already packed, given notice to the landlady, and bought a ticket to Ohio. He made many friends and would keep them. His working days in Washington were over but the friendships lingered for years.

Louisa had been alerted to his return. She and Elise had a serious disagreement shortly after their first discussion of the direction of the League of Women Voters. They agreed to consider a ban on free speech at home, which allowed them to keep their friendship intact.

Shortly before the extent of the crash was known, Roger Taft called a Board Meeting. Willie was not able to attend but he heard the bad news before the meeting was called to order. There was nothing to be done. Most of the capital invested in the new corporation had been moved into stocks. The business fostered by Wilhelm Knobholtz aka William Holtz was teetering on the edge of ruin. Louisa, Elise, and Emilia were told by Roger of the financial situation and of the possible dissolution of the corporation itself.

William was in the room during this conference. He seemed agitated but said nothing. The small group dispersed and Emilia and William went to bed. Emilia slept soundly, exhausted by the news. In the morning, William was not to be found. Emilia finally noticed a scrap of paper on the breakfast table. It read *Ich Bie Der Arbeit.*

"What does this mean," Emilia was crying. Strands of grey hair covered her forehead hiding eyes that no longer looked sightless. Greta came into the room, read the note and picked up the telephone. She was also crying when she said, "Elise, I believe your father has gone to the factory. He left a note that he was off to work and he is nowhere in the house."

He was found at the front entrance of the factory. He had been dead for several hours.

Part Three

The 1930's

Chapter 28

Adjustments

Willie was on the train, headed for Cincinnati. Louis met him with the car and he was soon in front of his sister's Clifton Avenue house. It was a different greeting than the last but he was welcomed as a resident rather than a visitor.

Before speaking to anyone at home, Willie had confirmed a position at the University. He would be teaching in the College of Commerce. Once home, the full impact of William's death was evident to Willie. Emilia was distraught, feeling that she had not been a good caregiver. Angelika and Greta felt the same. It took much comforting from Elise to assure them that it was not their lack of care but William's illness that took him out on the cold fall night.

Herman would be home that evening. He would have to be told that much of the family assets were gone along with their father.

The funeral was planned and a new grave in the cemetery readied for William. He would join Elise and Frank's stillborn daughter, Hilde, and the baby Louisa and Willie had lost soon after their marriage. It was a plot for the very old and the very, very young. Gathered around the open grave were William's wife, Emilia, his sons, Willie and Herman, and his daughter Elise. In the last months, he had not recognized any of them.

Over their years in Cincinnati, two immigrants from Germany had three children. Elise, the oldest, had three children who would most surely have children and the Holtz name would be honored for decades to come. William left a legacy of work and honesty that each would follow. In all, those attending his funeral numbered forty, counting family, household help, workers from the factory, members of his church and friends from the neighborhood.

All were invited to Elise's house and were received by the family. Emilia was warmed by the attendance. The last months had been difficult for her. William Holtz had been gone for a long time, replaced by a shadow that people recognized but did not know. His bodily presence remained, but the man who had high hopes for his business and his sons had left them many months ago.

Every hour he spent at the factory was done for his boys. After Elise married and the business became a part of F & B Industries, William was determined to leave plans that would move the company into the future. Emilia wondered how much of the last events he had understood. He knew he had to do something when he made that last trip to the workplace. Perhaps he knew there was nothing he could do.

It was the end of an era in many ways. It was difficult,

but no one brought up the question of business. There were a few tears but surely, they were for the man who had done so much for all of them. There are so many things that money can't buy.

Willie and Herman discussed their plans away from the family gathering. They fashioned a solution of sorts and it was accepted without question when they shared it later in the day. Louise was to rejoin Willie and live with Emilia in her house, near Elise but closer to campus. Willie's new job would start spring semester. He appreciated the easier commute. Washington traveling posed many problems for him and this would help his mobility and his dignity as well.

"If I never ride a train again I will be a happy man." This was Willie's answer to the new arrangements. Herman answered him by saying, "Yes, Willie, flying is much better."

A few days after the funeral, Greta, Elise, Willie, Louisa and the three Freimarck children accompanied Herman and Angelika to City Hall. The happy couple were married without the blessing of any church and counted themselves lucky to avoid the controversy a choice of religion would involve.

In the midst of packing and unpacking, Louis brought news. His sister had been cleared for entry, had disembarked at Ellis Island, and, if all went well, Sonia and her daughter Brigitte could soon be in Ohio. They were excited to build a new life in Cincinnati. For Sonia, it was the second time the city had opened its arms to her. This was the best news Elise had received in some time. Sonia was welcome to live in her home and she immediately began to assign space for them.

The Taft and Alden families aired criticisms of recent decisions in private discussions only. They heard a ripping noise in the fabric of the family. It was not long before they realized the value of being left out of some family business. And yet they were ready to mend the damage.

It was the first time that F & B Industries were not the full focus of everyone's thoughts. The exact status of the business was foggy, no one really knew if the newly formed corporation would survive. Investments proceeded in the past year although Willie advised a pull back. The full impact of recent bank failures needed to be assessed. Slowly, family members determined how an economic collapse would affect them personally.

Most of the family had been employed, and they had employed others. That needed reassessment. The four women refused to release those who had served them for so long. At the very least, they would have a home. Roger and Augusta pondered bringing Gertrude, John and their three daughters to live in their big Avondale house. The thought of three girls sharing his table did not make Roger happy. His only child, Charles, was at University. As planned, Charles was attending Harvard as his uncle Frank had done several years ago. It would be hard to justify two people living in the huge house even though they kept some of the staff who had no other home.

Harvard had already left Roger's mind. The state of their bank accounts was unknown. The ability of the business to pay Roger and John was a question mark.

It would be difficult to maintain their lifestyle on less pay. He was uneasy but not yet in panic mode. Until he remembered his responsibility to Elise and Frank's children, things had seemed under control. Considering their status gave him a jolt. They were all growing up and needed to find a profession.

One thing was certain; it would not be Yale or Harvard for William Frederick. He had enrolled in the University of Cincinnati, studying political science and hoping to transfer after two years. That was now impossible.

Willie made his new position known and there was a general cheer. Louisa was lauded for being employed as a teacher. Herman would not be a liability but an asset for the first time.

Elise recognized herself as the outlier. "I will also be able to contribute." She announced this although she had not decided to take the job offered. It paid little and was called a training slot. Her letter to the ACLU was received with pleasure. Elise had been asked to train as a paralegal for a Cincinnati Civil Rights lawyer.

"I hadn't the time to explain this but I will begin after the holidays. No salary has been mentioned and I will attend the College of Law for night school coursework. Willie and I will be on campus together this time." That thought was the one that made it worthwhile. She would not watch her brother come home with books and papers to read. She would not embroider. Maybe mend things, but no samplers. Elise would be a student again and that was better than a mid-life crisis.

One income was secure and if Louisa had her contract

renewed they would be able to scrape together a living for themselves. It was even possible that Herman could add some funds.

More than subsistence for the family, Willie worried about those who had served them well for years as cooks, cleaners, tutors, landscapers, and child watchers. They would now be unemployed, some of them at an age where no other employment could be found. Government assistance was discussed but not presently available. What would all the unemployed live on? This would be a problem for many University professors to grapple with in the coming months.

While the adults agonized over the possible loss of income, the next generation listened at doorways and near telephones. All were old enough to know some kind of catastrophe had occurred. They were exonerated. This time not one of them had brought disaster to the family. It was the economy.

Chapter 29

The Next Generation Grows

Rick waited for Willie. Willie smiled and said, "Hi Will!" He forgot that William Frederick Freimarck, named for his grandfather as Willie had been named for his father, was sick of being in a line of Williams and its derivatives. His name was Rick now and that is who he was.

"Sorry Will, I mean Rick! My mind is too full to remember anything else today. Is there something I can help you to understand? I am counting on you to keep your sister calm." Willie wasn't sure how to explain an economic crisis to a young person but willing to try. He will consider this while writing his new syllabus.

Rick began with the main problem. "Will we be able to stay in school? I have heard that Charles will stay at Harvard. Somehow. I don't think he has done a stellar job. Will the rest of us have to find employment?"

Willie was more than relieved. The first observation that came to him was: there are no jobs. It would be better to explain that predicament later. Willie answered, "You can thank God for public education, Frederick. You will all stay in school as planned. Only Charles will have fewer choices. There is one thing that will change and that is the lack of tutors and special help. You will all be expected to care for each other and yourselves. Can you do that?"

"I can do that, Uncle Willie, and to tell you the truth, I am pleased to take care of myself. I believe Mama has forgotten that children grow up." At best, he thought, we have moved on from Will to Frederick. Rick gave his uncle a hug and left to find Eva Emilia and Max and to call their cousins together. There would be another kind of meeting than the one at the house.

The youngest family members gathered together in the carriage house. It was the place to go when adult interference was unwanted. Charles was pacing along the back wall. The others sat on various auto parts and decaying carriages, looking cold and miserable. When Rick came in he made it a grand entrance: "All is fine. We will continue in school. Uncle Willie has promised."

Charles decided to take his cousin's message as a personal invitation to leave the meeting. He had a role in a theater production at University and was worried it would be handed to someone else if his absence was too lengthy. Sports were now a fall back for Charles; he found a home on stage.

Rick took charge and began to note the status of each of them. He had a plan of his own, one that had already been put in action. If it worked, he would hold another meeting. He looked around and saw few smiles but a ray of hope in each face. One of Aunt Gertrud's daughters was married and she would be under the charge of her husband's family, not this one. The other daughters were still in high school.

Eva Emilia did smile. "I am completing high school in June. I have a full scholarship to the College of Nursing at the University. Uncle Willie already checked and I am on the roster for September. The scholarships are from a foundation, dedicated to building a cadre of nurses in the city. It will not be erased but I will live at home instead of on campus." She did not mention her irritation with the smug acceptance of her skills in nursing as a fine career for a woman. Eva E. found she had more skills than she needed and she planned to continue her medical studies after her first degree. Not an issue to address today.

"Did Uncle Willie say anything about Walnut Hills?" Max was just qualifying for the advanced coursework in mechanical drawing. It was something he had looked forward to for many years. His grandfather had talked to him about it when he was still in short pants.

"No worries, Max, the high school is public and you are a good student. Brigitte, Sonia's daughter, and two of Aunt Gertrude's girls will all attend Walnut Hills with any luck.

"I am sorry to tell you that there will be no private tutors. You are on your own this term." Rick was not surprised to hear a cheer for this statement.

Max laughed. "We are heartily sick of our tutors, please don't tell Uncle, but this gives us more time to study what we know we should. My tutor had me reading books written a century past. Who cares what happened a hundred years ago?"

Rick looked around the group. They were remarkably attentive but he had no more to say. As far as he was concerned, all those needing an education had it. Cincinnati's public schools had come through once again.

Rick realized that he was the only mystery and in the general good will of the moment he decided to keep his hopes to himself. He had been seeking recommendations, he had obtained them, and his application to West Point was on its way. He hoped to join the aviation program there in the spring. He had taken extra coursework, advised by Uncle Herman, at the local Tech school before he entered the University of Cincinnati. The engineering courses he took prepared him for The Point. He was primed to fly with his Uncle Herman if his luck held and he was accepted.

Uncle Herman now lived in a Dayton suburb with his wife, Angelika. They had rented a small apartment, suitable for starting their new life. Each morning Herman left for the army base and his wife, to ensure good use of time, began searching for a true home. She had a secret to share with her husband and it influenced the house hunting: The new couple would become parents.

Angelika had parts of her life more traumatic than Herman. She saw her family dissolve before her eyes. They had been one of the most respected denizens of their small village, and then there were none left. When Angelika and Greta met Elise in the temporary camp hospital, they said good-bye to their mother, the last of the family. Without Elise, they would probably be gone as well. And now, Angelika was going to add to the Holtz family long after they had given up hope of Herman becoming a father.

Eva Emilia helped her find a physician in the Dayton area. The house was located on a quiet street with a fenced in yard. The last chore was almost complete. Angelika located a synagogue on Riverside Drive in Dayton. It was founded in 1850, before the Holtz family arrived. The members met in rented halls until The Temple Israel was built in 1873. The Temple belonged to the Union of Reform Judaism and it was a perfect fit for Angelika and Herman.

That night, Angelika finally responded when Herman asked, "What did you do today while I was at work?"

Her answer revealed the reason for a house.

They became members of the Temple and shortly after they became the parents of twin boys named Victor and Aaron. It was a time to rejoice and add a new branch to the family tree.

Chapter 30

Rising from the Ashes

President Hoover was labeled a financial genius. Surely this was the time for one in the White House. Unfortunately, his conservative slant made it impossible for him to use federal money to carry the nation through the great crash. When Franklin Delano Roosevelt took office in 1933, one hundred days of action began to ease the pain and true or not, Happy Days were announced. Hoover's corner was turned.

The most troubling of practices were addressed quickly. FDIC set up Federally backed insurance for deposits, the Federal Reserve was strengthened, a Home Owners law put the brakes on foreclosures, and the Federal Securities Act set regulations for stocks and trading. A New Deal was afoot.

This included public works, exemplified by the CCC and the WPA. The National Recovery Act, NRA, allowed for federal funding for massive projects that benefitted the nation and aided recovery. Agriculture was assisted through buy backs that limited surpluses and farmers began to climb out of the depths of depression. Only the

Dust Bowl is remembered as a tragedy of the times, a natural disaster that sent the Okies west.

Through poverty, hunger, migration to cities, bank failures and sickness, the people of America were able to see the rest of the world coping badly. Communism, fascism and capitalism were judged and the horrors of the Spanish Civil War shocked the nation. Newsreels showed the extent of cruelty in Russia, Italy, Germany and Spain as the decade progressed. The media exposed all and the policies of compassionate government won the public's support.

An International effort to combat Franco's fight to control Spain was formed. The Abraham Lincoln Brigade included some Americans who saw the horrors of war for the first time. Herman found the use of German bombs to subdue Guernica in the Basque region of Spain a compelling example of the need to improve aviation in America. He realized and brought information to the Army administrators in Dayton about the development of bombers in Germany. He made his point with the help of the German demonstration of the power of the airplane.

Another major adjustment came with the end of Prohibition. This was one of the first laws to be retracted. It had led to crime and a culture of gangsters, the St. Valentine's Day massacre, and a plethora of films depicting the underworld. The exploits of the Untouchables exposed the difficulties of convicting criminals of a crime, unless it involved unpaid taxes.

Willie Holtz, now a teaching Professor of Commerce, spent a great deal of time building a new curriculum.

Jean Romano

The old values of individual choices over the needs of the nation had undergone a change. Adam Smith was discarded; John Maynard Keynes won the day. In class, Dr. Holtz found few challenged the new views. All could clearly see that a global economy had replaced the vision of the solitary frontiersman holding the world at bay with only his horse and a Winchester rifle.

The first generation immigrants would have been astounded. Second generation Americans were learning their place in a different society. And the third generation had nothing to fear but fear itself.

The concentration on economic issues was overpowering. The other aspects of the decade helped alleviate the pain. Media was on the rise. Roosevelt conducted Fireside Chats on the radio. Broadcasters were available to be a companion at all times. Jazz continued to produce icons; literature shone, painters painted, and play writers put out their best. Even Musical Theater entered public consciousness. The movies were incredible examples of good acting, good plots and good escapes from the dreariness at home. Gangster movies of the ' 30's are classics over one hundred years later and so is Charlie Chaplin.

The rise of the arts especially attracted Charles Taft, Augusta's son. His affair with acting was encouraged by the Federal Theater Project. He now had a destination when and if his last year at University would end. He did not share his plans with any family member. His cousins talked of ideas he felt beneath him. He would have a presence felt around the planet.

The Melting Pot: 1919-1939

Charles looked remarkably like his Uncle Frank. It frightened his mother. He had religiously followed Frank's footsteps to a point and then realized there was no need to do so. Uncle Frank was a no show now; he said he was in Germany but who knew? As Charles remarked to his mother, "What news from Uncle Frank? Has he been elected to office in Germany? I hear the Weimar Republic is shaky, that sounds to me like the Uncle I know and love has been busy, politically speaking."

Augusta was in no mood to humor Charles at this point. Your grandmama would be devastated to hear you speak so lightly of Frank! He was a model for us all and he made the business solvent and then flourishing! Watch how you speak of him to the others." Augusta was careful not to condemn Frank until the terms of the Will were fully explained to her. When she saw her son she sometimes felt he was Frank! That was a worrisome thought.

"Mama, I am sure you do not know that Frank's stay in Germany was not his choice. I am a good listener at keyholes and Uncle Willie has set out a picture of Dorian Grey in the disguise of an Ohio businessman. He couldn't come home if he wanted to and he doesn't want to now. Elise is the head of the family and she might even lock the door if she saw him coming!"

Augusta blanched. She did not know that Charles had heard the gossip floating around the name Frank. "Well, manage your own affairs better. Your father and

I are interested in your next move. Please, don't let it be Cincinnati!"

And it was not. Charles found dropping out of University a better idea than finding a job to pay tuition for a life he didn't enjoy. Over the past year he had saved enough money to make the trip to Hollywood. He was scheduled for a screen test in early spring. The date coincided with the start of the new semester but Harvard would survive without Charles Taft. His name belonged in lights.

The next closest cousins also had plans. Gertrud's oldest daughter, Mary, was expecting a baby at any moment. "At least someone in the family is doing what they are supposed to do." Gertrud was happy with the marriage – one settled and two to go.

The next cousin, Frederick or Rick, was Frank's son in name only. While he had the family's physical grace, his hair and eyes were dark brown, he had shaved off his moustache and dressed to be ready to run, jump, or tackle someone at any moment. He was concerned with physical fitness, one of the requirements for The Point. He had two years of college and was under twenty-five. It was now or never. The letter of acceptance came shortly before Easter break. Rick was not sure how to break the news. Uncle Willie, who helped with contacts, and Uncle Herman who gave advice, both knew he had applied. The three celebrated together before spreading the good news. "It was worth the effort." Rick was content to leave it there. He would join the new cadets in May.

As it happens in every family, there is a period of

growth and a slow leaking away of the whole over time. Of course, Mary's baby would make up for the loss of Charles. "More than make up, it is an extremely pleasant addition and a joyous subtraction!" Almost all of the cousins were delighted to wish Charles luck and to kiss him good-bye.

Rick was another story. He kept them all informed, helped when needed, and soothed the parents when something went wrong. Max would feel the loss of his brother the most. He had no real connection to Charles and didn't share Rick's goals in any way. He depended on his brother for advice and support. There was no one to take his place. When he thought about it he realized that he was closest to his mother. They shared an interest in politics, civil rights battles, and reform. Elise and Max had a Sunday night ritual that involved hot chocolate and heated discussions. They parted each session fully satisfied that they had won whatever argument was the topic of the date.

Eva Emilia was aware of the males in the family, uninterested in the other female cousins and sure of her own ability to fulfill her promise to her grandmother. She enrolled in the College of Nursing because it was the best route to proceed to her real goal. Of all the children, she was the one to receive scholarships, honor grades, and praise from the professionals. As she and her Grandmama Emilia planned, Eva E. would not become a nurse, she would continue on until her credentials clearly named her Doctor Holtz. Eva E. looked forward to showing that paper to Emilia.

Elizabeth and Jane Alden, daughters of Gertrud, were still undecided. They were in awe of Eva E. and so there was no true relationship. Their mother and father assumed they would marry and raise grand children. They were not sure but did not feel equal to a family discussion. Brigitte came under their spell and the three girls tried out possible futures in the carriage house hideaway. How fortunate it was not wired for sound.

And so the third generation spread their wings and looked back on the ' 30's as a good time despite the hardships. The biggest event was the birth of Mary's baby son. Emilia was at the hospital before Mary. She was waiting in the hallway when Mary arrived with her husband, and it was Emilia who went with her to the labor room. It was not an easy birth but the moment was a happy one. Emilia was the messenger who brought the news to the father, a young and nervous University student who had not planned on fatherhood so soon. Emilia's blessings washed over him and he was able to meet his first child with love.

When Emilia returned home she was tired and achy. "I am getting too old for hospital duties." It would pass and she would rest tomorrow. By the next day, Emilia could not leave her bed. A few days later she was diagnosed with pneumonia. And a few days after the diagnosis this very strong and dedicated woman died at home. She refused to go to the hospital.

Chapter 31

Moving On

The Sunday Breakfast Table Chats between Elise and Max continued. They both missed Emilia but only Elise knew the extent of her mother's impact. She determined to write an obituary that would last and give her the honor she deserved. Forgotten were the grievances over the role of women and the subservience of daughter to mother. Emilia had overcome that myth herself.

"Max, we will leave your Grandmama's legacy for Eva Emilia to follow. I believe she is keeping her plans secret to ward off any negative comments about women as doctors." Elise really wanted to know what her youngest son was thinking.

Max smiled. "Mama, both Eva and I decided we would be tempting fate to announce our plans too early. Luckily, I am not sure about mine. And so, it is my turn to talk to you, not as a mother, but as a guide to next steps."

"Very well. You may have noticed that I have learned not to give unsolicited advice. In fact, I could not have given this advice a few months ago. Max, I love my new tasks. I make little money but my educational needs are paid for and when finished, my salary will increase. I am not pleased because I have a paycheck. I am content because I will someday earn it. And Max, I am completely satisfied with the work I can do."

That was a long speech for Elise and she did not often lecture. Max was impressed with the intensity his mother allowed to show. She had been dedicated to immigrant paths to citizenship, the treatment of immigrants, and then the discrimination against women. She was totally involved with a broader picture now. The discrimination she and the family had endured on arrival and during the war years was the core of her mission to end discrimination in any form. And it was very evident in Cincinnati, a city on the borders of north and south.

Max was not sure how his mother's passion affected him. So she told him. "Max, there is a lack of lawyers in the field of civil rights. The Civil War ended slavery but it enflamed those who lost the battle. States are making laws that are clearly unconstitutional. The 14th Amendment is clear but disregarded. And as for our African-Americans, yes, they are hyphenated too, move north, they see discrimination at every turn. It is in segregated housing, employment, public accommodations and worst of all, in our country's public schools. The laws need to be made and if already on the books, enforced."

Elise stopped to note Max's reaction. It was all she could want. "Mama, I can see why you are working so hard. Not to provide food and shelter but to advance the values of America." He decided that sounded a little pretentious but Elise was pleased. This Sunday had started her son on a new pathway.

Elise had been reading the works of Du Bois and regretted missing the debate in Chicago. Another time. When working for Women's Suffrage, the largest surprise was the increased number and diversity of new people attending the local meetings. Not only the German community but also Irish, Russian, Jewish and a few African-Americans began to fill the auditorium seats. The lack of warmth of some towards the Black women bothered her more and more. She had argued with Louisa over the issue, causing a break in their relationship. And it was still at the top of her agenda. Elise decided that approaching Louisa was the best move she could make.

'If I can't explain myself to Louisa Freimarck, I cannot hope to reach anyone else." This gave her the urgency needed to try her change of plan.

And so the two met for a chat that same week, after Louisa returned from school. She was teaching fourth grade, the time when children are supposed to read to learn, not to decipher words. Louisa was unhappy with the difference in progress between white and black students. This meant she was working overtime to identify why there were gaps and what to do about them. It was the perfect time for Elise and Louisa to evaluate a course of action.

Elise asked Louisa where the children in her classroom lived. Louisa wasn't sure. It was soon clear that housing concentrated new immigrants from Europe in one area of the city, old time residents in a separate district, and

African=Americans, even if citizens by birth, in still another. In some states property zoning was set by law. In Cincinnati the Black Codes were discarded but segregation appeared to remain by custom. Elise determined to check on this.

"How much does poverty affect learning?" Elise was curious. Did colleges of education ever study the results of poverty on learning? She had heard the phrase "separate but equal" more than once and in many contexts. Did it apply to public education as well?

For the first time Elise held Louisa's attention. She knew the classroom was not the determinant of success or failure. And she was learning through the League that having the legal ability to vote does not automatically result in casting a ballot. For many reasons, and because States created their own rules, African-Americans could be denied the vote. Not voting meant not having a voice in the city, the state or the nation.

At the Law Offices where Elise was employed, the current talk involved due process for the rights of non-citizens and the affect of racial discrimination on the rights of African=Americans.

"These should be causes to ensure there are idealists to dedicate themselves to the issues over the next hundred years." Elise spoke and for the first time, Louisa smiled.

The two parted friends again. Neither changed their focus, but each respected the vision of the other. They held the same goals but had different paths to achieve them. They agreed to meet weekly.

"I will have to set up a calendar!" Elise was delighted by the thought.

Willie's reaction to Louisa's report on her meeting with his sister was one of quiet joy. These were the favorite members of the family for Willie. He no longer felt that his tutorials were needed from him; they were totally immersed in their own research.

Chapter 32

Changes of Procedure

Franklin Delano Roosevelt was inaugurated in 1933. Albert Einstein immigrated to America in the same year and became a citizen three years later. When Einstein met FDR, he warned that the Nazi run government might be developing nuclear weapons. There was also a letter from Leo Szilard, a Hungarian refugee, with the same message. The resulting Manhattan Project probably saved America and it most surely accelerated the end of World War II. The number of scientists fleeing Germany, many of them Jewish, was large enough to be called a brain drain.

If anything prompted a reassessment of education in America it was this. William and Emilia could have given testimony about education in Germany. It had focus. The outcomes were determined by national need. The best were elevated to higher more intense studies early in their school years; the others were identified for future jobs and trained accordingly.

Company towns operated all that was needed for a comfortable life. Hospitals, stores, schools, and churches were available to workers in a defined district or to those employed by a specific industry. The workers worked, the children were trained to take their place but at a higher level of technical skill. Children showing aptitude in math or science were treated well. Teachers were outstanding. Of course, there were caveats, such as limitations on political beliefs or freedom of speech. No communists need apply. Some things were not to be questioned and discipline was strict. It was one of the reasons Wilhelm Knobholtz became William Holtz.

Louisa was a certified teacher through the University of Cincinnati's College of Education. Slates had been replaced with pencil and paper. The blackboard served as a reminder of how far the profession had come. The slow integration of the public schools was evident in Louisa's classroom and she decided to make home visits to learn more about her struggling students. This did not change her views on women's suffrage; it still appeared the best way to change the laws and to get assistance for families in need. After her meeting with Elise, she was ready to admit that women needed to be involved in making the laws as well. They would each address one part of the problem. For Louisa now, it was determining a way to raise achievement for her African=American children to give them a chance to pass the test for entry to Walnut Hills and then College. Geographically speaking, Walnut Hills was their neighborhood school.

Her next step was to enlist Willie and she did this in a peaceful moment. "Willie, do you have a way to determine how many black graduates are recorded from the University? Or better, how many are there now? I have been thinking of a program to bring them to speak to our students in elementary school. Their stories should be inspiring."

"Louisa, yes. I can probably find the numbers and names through the Admissions Office. You must know that the African-American students do have issues on campus. They are not accepted in all areas. To continue, they develop a strong core belief in their worth and mission and they have started an organization to help each other and to protest discrimination. You might think more than once about bringing them into public schools. It could hurt the school, the teachers, and worst of all, it could be harmful to the College students." Willie was aware of the need for scholarship funding, the reputation of the University, the possible wrath of some white parents, and administrative fall-out for Louisa. The most amazing part to Willie was the acceptance of discrimination that continued even as more black students were enrolled.

"Let's ask the students how they feel, Willie. And I will check with both my principal and the School Superintendent. If there is even a tinge of rejection for my idea, I will find another way to approach my concerns." Louisa was satisfied that something would happen. Anything would be better than nothing at all and Louisa always chose to do two jobs herself rather than ask another to help her.

The perfect person appeared. She was put in touch with a black graduate of the University who then completed his studies at the University College of Law. He was a practicing Attorney and involved in the Cincinnati Branch of the NAACP. There could not possibly be a better person to contact.

John Alden, brother=in=law to Elise, was also a graduate of the College of Law in Cincinnati. He heard of the contact Louisa made and congratulated her. In fact, he made an effort to seek her out in order to congratulate her. John had entered the merger of F & B Industries with a larger corporation as the attorney for F & B affairs. As a lawyer, this gave him the schedule for his employment. It would not be lengthy. Once the merger was running smoothly, he would be looking for another position. Roger was on the Board of Trustees by contract and that could last for some years. He was expendable.

John had come to F & B because of Eva's investment and his credentials as a lawyer, but his actual experience was slight. Life had been good to him and then he had married well. It made him chuckle to think of immigrant families looking to better themselves by advantageous marriages. He had managed his search for a bride well and he loved Gertrud. One boy out of three children would have been better but he was not sexist. Or racist. In fact, John was ready to get along with anyone and he saw possibilities through Elise's work as a paralegal and now Louisa's connection to a rising African-American star in the city.

"I can't think why they are still called African=American. I have heard Negro, colored, black and worse. It is time to just call all the hyphenated citizens Americans." Perhaps because of never needing to compete,

John held few grievances for minorities at this point. He was much more affected negatively by those with differing political views.

Before sleeping that night, John looked up information on the NAACP, was satisfied and decided to pursue a connection there. Maybe sooner rather than later made more sense.

The country and the family had made a move to the left. It wasn't opportunism; it was the way history indicated was right. It was time for all good men and women to come to the front lines and to put country before them selves. If this helped them personally, it was the will of the gods. John retired early and slept soundly.

Willie was the last to sleep after Louisa reported her talk with John. Willie knew that there was a man searching for employment on the loose. "And what of it? He has grown a lot in the past four years and constantly surprises me. His grasp on the economy is good. I have had better talks with him than with Roger. If he is open to International Law including human rights he might fit into the coming decades well. Louisa, good for you. Next chat will be for three."

Louisa rolled over and turned on the light. "Willie, you are taking this all far too seriously. Sleep on it." She turned off the light.

Chapter 33

The Unexpected is Certain

Elise had a spotty career as a mother. When she was very young, she was convinced by her mother that all life asked of her was to marry well. This was accomplished and she wondered what to do next. Her entry into high society was unsuccessful. The Cincinnati Symphony was her first venture into the role of society matron and it did not go well. Until she met Tom Johnson, on the voyage to Germany, no one except her brothers' tutors had noticed she had a brain. They were glad to concentrate their efforts on the pretty girl who was interested in poetry and literature rather than her siblings who were only interested in railroads and engines.

In later years, she blessed Tom for leaving her with no signs of sadness. He explained in few words the importance of a moment in time that has to be cherished but not extended. Love was not part of his attraction to her and the trip had been lucrative for him. He was surprised to find that Elise saw their relationship differently. The moment effectively shielded Elise from further emotional mistakes.

Max was the youngest of Elise's children. She did raise Max. Her mother-in-law finally ceded the rights to the children to their mother but too late for Will/Frederick/ Rick and Eva Emilia to be affected. Rick became attached to Uncle Herman and Eva E. was devoted to her grandmother Emilia. Elise's weekly chats with Max centered on what he was learning and then sharing what she had learned. She became interested in Max as a person who shared her vision and he became intrigued with the law and social justice.

Max was admitted to the University of Cincinnati College of Law on the basis of his grades and a recommendation from his Uncle Willie. He also received a scholarship. For many years he had followed his brother's fascination with flight. His interest had changed for several reasons. One was his mother's dedicated work on civil rights, and the other, a girl he met in high school. She was active in NAACP and determined to become an attorney. At first Max saw her as a feminine version of his Uncle John. Each year they grew older, that comparison faded more. She was beautiful and smart. She was black. He loved her.

The two joined the same study group, attended NAACP meetings together, and joined the Student organization Quadres. Max stood out in the group because he was "different" but he was never asked to leave. They couldn't. With a goal of interracial harmony, Max was proof of its possibility,

Elise accepted Letitia with open arms. Even before it was obvious to Max, his mother the bond between the two was much more than one of classmates. Elise felt exactly the same about the young woman and was proud of her son's choice. What she saw ahead was a lifetime of trouble for them and for any children they might have. This was part of the picture she would let them discover on their own. "They are young, they are sure of the righteousness of their cause. They will realize this is a friendship to preserve forever, or they will make the commitment that will change their lives." Elise left this topic out of the Sunday talks.

Louisa had invited Elise to join her at the annual Teachers' Convention in Cleveland. It seemed possible and the cost small. Elise decided to plan a delegation of duties to Sonia, Greta, and Louis. She would go. Only one small hesitation came to mind. Her cat. The one living thing who stood by her in all crises and who was grateful for a pat on the head and an occasional kipper was her cat.

"I will write specific directions for Sonia. Or maybe, Brigitte will take on this responsibility." Elise sat down to write directions.

INSTRUCTIONS FOR GRETL THE CAT

Dislikes: Noise

Inside: Do not play loud music on the radio while she is present.

Outside: Do not use lawn mower in her hearing range. If possible, ask the neighbors to observe the same restrictions.

Low-flying planes must be admonished.

Risks

Inside: Preference is for sleeping across the middle steps of stairs by the outer wall. Do not attempt to go down or upstairs in the dark. Gretl enjoys finding new places for sleep and grooming activities, be careful where you step. She has no fixed routine so look before you sit down. Some chairs are more attractive than others.

Menu Suggestions

No one who is a basic gourmet likes to eat the same meal over and over. Do not repeat a "favorite" as she will immediately decide the selection is in poor taste. Her water bowl is kept fresh and full but her preference is for her own glass on the upstairs bathroom counter.

Social Events

Company is forbidden.

Animal Friendships

Gretl enjoys playing with mice. They do not enjoy it. She also has a pet squirrel who lives inside the walls of the house. A local grey cat is unacceptable, a wandering Siamese is a friend. Does not like bears, raccoons, possums or deer. Turkeys are also on the not welcome list. Dogs should not be mentioned aloud but she enjoys observing them bark when locked up inside their own houses.

Good Luck! I know they all will be quite attached to her when I return! Elise decided to stock up on cat food to make it easier for Brigitte. The cat knew she was the subject of attention and swished her tail.

The two women would be gone only one night. Louis drove them to the station for the short train ride. Dormitory rooms at the University had been located for the visitors. It would be a weekend to remember.

The Call to Order next morning began a frustrating and unproductive conference. Teachers, all women, trailed in from the dorms the University assigned for the group. They looked rumpled and hungry, just like most of the students they served at home. Some were looking for programs and finding none, they approached the registration desks to ask for a schedule. All of those assembled were organized and on task in their classrooms and disappointed in the chaos they found at a professional meeting.

The organizers, trying to gain the attention of government officials, were not. They had tried but found little support for any upgrades to the funding of public education in Ohio. The most common reply: "Perhaps next year." It was clear that public schools were not on the A list yet.

Elise found her only interest was in finding out how Ohio was trending on ending segregated schools and what measures were being taken to equalize public education. Not many, funds had been frozen and innovation was slow. The new President was a friend of the poor but not the other "elite" students. His opinion of teachers requiring certification was low. His intention of funding new school buildings: zero. This was understandable but not uplifting for those facing needy children on a daily basis.

Elise and Louisa were much more involved in talks with teachers who were buying supplies for their classrooms despite their own scanty and reduced salaries. Louisa noted a definite reaction to separate but equal and determined to put education in a primary position for League of Women Voters agenda.

The emphasis on literacy, science and agricultural technique was a repeat of the remarks of the past year. Specifics were hard to come by and funding even less possible. Even research at Universities had lost federal funding.

And so the two women left with many contacts that might become comrades in arms. They learned little new because there was very little new. The good will and passion for education off=set the lack of good news. They found that federal funds were diverted to the mass of unemployed, not the future unemployed.

Again, it was the economy. Slowly the depression was ending and the education of the country's youngest would be a priority again. Louisa remarked that Willie had it all figured out. Elise was sure he had. And then they rushed to the station for the early train home.

Louis met them at the station. "How is everything at home?" Elise asked this expecting to hear "Fine" as an answer.

"Don't ask." This was the cryptic response they would have to live with until they reached Clifton Avenue.

Sonia met them without her usual happy smile.

Elise decided the cat had proven troublesome. "Where is Gretl?" As she asked the cat came running. Now Elise was sure her absence had caused the disruption. "I am so sorry, Sonia. I will speak to Puss and promise not to leave again!"

"I wish it were the cat, madam. It is far worse. Charles has left school.'

:"As if he would ever have graduated, he had been claiming an advanced degree and he was close to thirty years old! True, he had a part time job producing student plays but it could hardly be called a career." Elise kept this under her breath. "He was sure to leave soon anyway, Sonia. His family may even be glad to hear this."

"Elise, Charles has left school and his destination is Hollywood! And he has taken Brigitte with him!" Sonia dissolved after this was communicated. It was not a bad thing to find Charles had moved on. Brigitte was her daughter and the best part of her life.

She had all of Elise's sympathy now. "Charles must have something in mind. Your daughter was attracted to him on his last visit home for Emilia's funeral. I did know that they were corresponding. Brigitte is much younger but she is also ambitious. Try to look at the possible good outcome! Maybe they will both find success?"

"That would be a great surprise." Sonia began to cry again and then she left Elise alone with her cat.

Elise now knew what Louis had meant with his short

response. This was his family too and he would feel the pain of his sister's loss.

Louisa came into the room, looking for Louis. She had gone directly home to check on Emilia. All was calm at Emilia's house. Too calm. "What is wrong, Emilia?" Louisa took the old woman's hands in hers. "Is Greta here? You are not alone?" Emilia shook her head and then put her arms around Louisa.

Again came the words Elise had said. "I am so sorry." Emilia cried. Then she delivered her news and they cried together. "Willie, has been called to Washington. They are trying to locate Frank. His name has come through to the Agency where they both worked and it is critical that they find him."

Louisa had been thinking about Frank. She and Elise never spoke of him unless it regarded the children, the current financial situation, or his lack of communication. In the last month or so, neither had spoken of him at all. His sisters, Augusta and Gertrud, had been asked what they had heard without admitting his wife had no letter or call. Not one person in the family or business had contact with Frank. As she went over what she knew and how little it was Louisa was walking towards Elise's house.

She opened the door to a scene of despair. Sonia and Louis were sitting together while he tried to stop her tears. Elise held her cat and tried to stay still. Louisa guessed that all those tears were not for Frank or even Willie.

Chapter 34

Trip to Germany

Willie was packing once again. "I should consider the suitcase my permanent bureau and save time." He was unhappy with his assignment but had no choice. The University not only wished him safe journey, they were thrilled to have a faculty member on a government mission.

The era of free trade died. Even if a product or commodity could be obtained at less cost from another country, self-sufficiency was the code word that stopped that practice. Tariffs were high and going higher. Only Spain had higher tariffs than America. And America was now a creditor nation while the former leaders were in debt. Many nations had abandoned the gold standard and the paper in use had little stability only ease of production.

A strong spirit of nationalism and isolation from other countries followed the unity reached at the close of the war. America was keeping Europe afloat with private investors providing the basis of Germany's reparations. When the crash forced investors to call in outstanding loans, the results were disastrous. As all nations put their efforts into increasing exports, the problem with gold and silver reserves became apparent.

At any rate, the Department of Commerce wanted to know exactly what state the German economy was in at this point. Some said it was nearing the production of America. How could this be? Willie was to find out through his contact with Frank. Apparently, no one had considered that Frank was not in constant contact with his Ohio family.

Louisa leaned on the door, watching her unhappy husband folding shirts. "Willie, I will fold the shirts and trousers. You find your personal needs. Greta is overseeing the laundry and it will be here in minutes. And I must let you know, half of the household and at least that many in the city of Cincinnati are writing notes for you to take to their families in Germany. And they do not have addresses, just names."

Her purpose was accomplished. Willie was aghast. "How on earth can I to deliver unaddressed missives across the country?"

"We will tell them, when you return, that the Central Post Office has the notes and will deliver them as addresses are confirmed. Honestly, it doesn't matter. You are giving hope to a great many people. They have been out of touch for so long. Even if you just put them in a post box the thought is there."

"Very well, Louisa, you are thinking ahead of me as usual. Please do not tell me that Elise has written to Frank." Willie stopped folding socks and looked at his wife. He saw the composed and thoughtful face he held in his heart for many years. He did not want to leave her now.

Louisa laughed and stopped folding shirts. "I am afraid that will not happen no matter how long it takes you to pack! Please, Willie, find him so we can have something to tell the children. Make something up if you have to, make Frank strong and useful, needed but sad to be away."

"I shall, Louisa. You are so wise." Greta brought the last of his garments, they packed them, shut the suitcase and kissed good-bye. Willie did not tell his wife of his mission as it was complicated by rules he had forgotten. Best to just go and return.

In fact, Willie had been asked to find out what products was the priority in Germany. Since the Ruhr had been returned, the factories there were noticeably busy. American analysts felts strongly that those factories were not turning out vacuum cleaners and washing machines. It had been rumored that the capital wealth of the country was allocated by the State. The Four Year Plan was known and sounded doubtful to the peace of the world. The Plan was designed to make Germany economically self-sufficient and militarily prepared. The question for Willie was what they were preparing for this time.

Germany's leadership in science was becoming better known with the immigration of people like Albert Einstein. But the scientific advances already known made the thrust of their research frightening. The last information gleaned in Washington described a new Germany with no trade unions, restricted media freedom,

University admittance for elite German only, and private capital under the guidance of the Central State. The government-distributed manpower where needed, made investments in the correct industries, and set both prices and wages for all goods and employers.

Willie was to sort this out and report back with a plan for American commerce and trade. He sank down into his coach seat and adjusted his leg brace. "This is surely a job for a man with two legs."

—⁓ ⁓—

Willie used his time on shipboard to write a paper. He was trying to expose the use of high tariffs as a barrier to economic growth and the challenge put him to sleep each night. Unfortunately, it would eventually put many readers to sleep. He enjoyed the sound of the moving ship and the smell of salt air.

The last time he had such a trip he had left Herman in Germany. Each hour further away from his brother that voyage was agony and he was sure he would never see him again. He was still in awe of Herman's recovery. On the other hand, he had been reasonably sure he would never see Frank again and it was a possibility that he would. In a way he would find that acceptable. Life had so many surprises. It is not wise to predict outcomes.

He found Frank by accident on the night of his arrival. Stiff and tired, he approached the desk at the hotel chosen for him. The manager told him they had no reservation in his name and no room open at all.

Polite, proper and persistent Willie raised his voice, and in mostly forgotten German announced that was impossible. The manager also raised his voice. Before the quarrel reached Wagnerian proportions, a man intervened.

"Otto," the voice said, "you have a guest from across the ocean. How unfriendly can you be? Let us show him how hospitality is done in Berlin."

The voice sounded familiar. Willie turned to face Frank who was leaning on the counter and smiling. "I recognized your German, Willie. It has a mid-western accent."

Of course a room was located and Willie's bag sent up. Frank and Willie retired to the lounge where Frank introduced him to a lady who looked very much like Elise but perhaps younger. It was not Elise.

"Willie, may I introduce you to my niece Clara?" Frank did not stammer or hesitate. Willie thought it might possibly be his niece.

"On which side of the family?" Willie could think of nothing more to say. They all were silent until Frank picked up the baton.

"Clara is related to the Freimarck family through my uncle. I am staying with them now as they have relocated to Berlin." Frank smiled and put an arm around his niece. They certainly looked like family. "We will get together later to catch up on things in Cincinnati. When will you feel ready for that, Willie?"

Willie responded "never" but only in his head. This was not the time to discuss the family across the ocean.

"Let us meet tomorrow morning. Is this the best place to have a breakfast meeting?"

And so the time and place were confirmed and Frank escorted his niece out of the lobby and into a waiting taxi.

Chapter 35

Catching Up and Watering Down

The two met the next day. Willie had many questions, Frank had few answers. Willie felt obligated to explain that his trip was under orders from the Department of Commerce and he had been charged to bring specific information back to Washington.

Frank diverted the conversation to ask about Elise, William Frederick, Eva Emilia, and Max. He was astounded that Frederick was enrolled at West Point. So much so that he was speechless for several minutes. "How did he manage that?"

This allowed Willie to explain the recommendations and Frederick's preparation for entry into the aviation program at The Point. He went on to describe Eva E's remarkable progress in the School of Medicine at the University. His last up-date concerned Max and his tentative step into the School of Law. In all, it was a record for family success, none of it due to their father's support.

"And Elise? Is she still concerned with voter registration

and women's rights? Has she cut off her hair once again?" Frank still saw Elise as the insecure and ineffectual girl he had married so many years past.

"She is a certified paralegal now, and working for a Civil Rights Law firm in the city. Her contacts were instrumental in Max's entry to Law School. You might be surprised to talk with her now, her goals have expanded and she is more than ready to work to achieve them." Willie felt confident that he had given Elise the credit she deserved. He was her ally now and would not let her be dismissed easily.

Frank could be seen thinking. His cigarette dropped ash on the table, his coffee cooled, and he had pulled his tie awry. He knew that the purpose of the meeting would require all of his wit and word power to deny, deflate and deter Willie from finding out what he had come so far to find: a picture of German industry.

The night before, Frank spoke to his superiors who, he found, already knew of Willie's arrival. They had also guessed what he wanted to know. Frank was under strict instructions to ensure he left knowing very little of what was happening in Germany.

"Let me tell you what I do, Willie, and you will have a better idea of what the state of German industry is now. I am living with the Freimarck family and have been employed by the government through their recommendations. You know how many years I worked for our Ohio business to foster exports to Germany. I had many contacts to begin with and it has been a joy to reconnect. And that is my job. The government has launched a plan of social reforms and the building of infrastructure. To ensure this plan will be expedited, the government uses oversight of industry to assure progress is steady. The Ruhr is now German once again but the disruption caused by the punitive treaties stifled their efforts for some time. Germany is recovering well. I can attest to that."

"We have knowledge of the Four Year Plan. Self-sufficiency seems to be the goal of many nations now. Can you tell me what the focus of production might be in the coming years?" This was as close as Willie chose to go with his questions now. He had a strong feeling that whatever he asked would be reported to others in the German government.

"I am sorry Willie. Specifics are beyond my knowledge. I will tell you that buildings, roads, stadia, post offices and such are all priorities. You know that my expertise is wrapped around the retooling of factories to expand their products and make them future friendly. Is that helpful?" Frank felt this would go well on Willie's report. He also hoped that his brother-in-law recognized that he would get no further information.

Willie did understand exactly what was happening. He had been briefed and knew that Germany was rearming, despite the Treaty of Versailles. Krupp was firmly in government hands and Gustav Krupp had been named Fuehrer of Industry. That was only one of many signals as the private companies were swept into the Central Government's plans. Willie realized he would learn nothing from Frank. He also noted that Frank had a few beads of sweat on his forehead and this was very unlike Frank who never sweated any confrontation.

The table in the lounge was full of crumbs, the ashtray was full of ashes. It certainly was a good metaphor for Willie's assignment. He assured Frank that his whereabouts and occupation were shared with Elise and his children. He would bring them Frank's love.

The conversation was shorter than expected. The room they sat in had lost most of its breakfast guests, only three or four well-dressed gentlemen remained in the room with the two gentlemen of Ohio. Willie guessed they were not there to eat breakfast.

When they parted, it was with relief on both sides.

Willie began packing once again. His entry visa did not allow him to travel freely. He had given his reason for the trip as a family visit to Frank and that was completed. The trip home would give him the time to write his report. In fact, he had learned more from the newspapers and radio than from his meeting. The National Socialist Party published extensively. Pamphlets were delivered door to door and airplanes showered towns and cities with additional pamphlets. The party printed more than one hundred newspapers and periodicals. The primary publication being the *Volkiche Beohochte* available everywhere. Willie searched news kiosks in a vain search for publications not bearing the stamp of the Nazi party.

New buildings were visible everywhere. The roads

were superb. And young men in brown shirts filled the streets looking fit and purposeful. Germany was prosperous and unemployment at its lowest point. While Frank discussed reforms to help the people, Willie noted the heralding of German spirit. It pervaded Berlin and pictures of Adolph Hitler were evident as well. Several recent immigrants with maximum security, briefed Washington about the status of military weaponry. Washington knew of the emphasis on the science related to warfare, the growth of the German Luftwaffe, the expansion of the factories of Krupp and others, and the increase of troops. Willie heard none of this from Frank. All of it was illegal through the terms of the Treaty of Versailles. He had learned more just by being present than by his meeting.

Willie knew that Frank was under pressure. He seemed to be trying to let him know that what he said was closely monitored. And he didn't have a drink while they were together. Willie did not think highly of Frank when he arrived, but he felt more worried than angry at him when he left for the trip home. He had fulfilled his charge, badly it seemed, but Willie had really been sent as a confirmation of what was already known. He never saw Frank again.

The Rhineland had more significance when he returned home. It was rich with the wines of the country, but it also held the coal that would build the nation into a military machine. Willie had been close to his father and knew without a refresher that it was a place of industry and talent. Production would be outstanding and the ability of the government to supply workers would add the needed boost. He had a moment of silence to thank his father for the foresight he showed in the past century. Willie was not sure how he would be placed in Germany now.

Chapter 36

Home Again

Willie was relieved that he did not have to report to Eva. Frank's mother had passed away some years before his trip. Elise would have his full attention and he would tell her only what he was sure was true. If Frank had a problem he could share, he would have done so. It seemed he preferred to deal with it on his own. It was easier to talk to his contacts in Washington than his family, and he did it well.

Elise wasn't sure what would happen if Frank decided to return with Willie. There was something about Willie, first Herman and now Frank had refused to make the trip back with him. Frank was alive and happy. She could live with that and she wished him well. Elise discarded all the grievances of the past during Frank's absence. She took her share of blame and forgave the sins of others. Her immersion in the law firm gave her hope each day that some injustices could be corrected.

The job at the law firm was settled. She had completed course work and was competent, punctual and willing to learn new procedures. More and more, clients of the firm's lawyers asked to speak to Elise first. She guided them to the specifics of their problem but listened to long stories the lawyers were not interested in hearing. She attended all firm meetings, ostensibly to take notes but they were all glad to have her there. One by one, most would ask her opinion of a case or a client when they were alone. And Elise kept a professional appearance. She dressed like the feminine version of a lawyer. No longer young, her appearance inspired confidence.

For this reason, Willie asked her to accompany him when he spoke to their brother, Herman who had just returned from visiting Frederick at West Point. The visit lasted longer than planned. Frederick continually talked about his uncle to the point, at The Point, that many doubted anything he said. The conclusion of Herman's visit would be a brief lecture of his interest in flying, his experience in Germany, and his current job with the Army. Herman was a smash. Now home, he was pleased that his nephew had carefully researched requirements, garnered recommendations, and made it into the prestigious program. He was training to be a pilot, just as his Uncle Herman had, but on the right side of the Atlantic.

Sitting down with Willie was an anti-climax but he promised himself that he would be polite. Herman was visibly shaken by the end of the visit,. Elise had not seen him so pale since their meeting at the Canadian hospital.

"Does this mean what I think? Will we be investigated as communicating with a possible enemy? Is Frederick in jeopardy?" Herman was upset and showed it.

"It would help if I answer one question at a time,

Herman. And be calm. Remember, I was in Germany at the request of the American government. I had an official role, not a family one. Both Frank and I were careful not to tread on shaky ground. So you do not need to shake now." Willie did not mention that he was also worried.

"It appears that Frank is assigned to oversee the conversion of factories to armaments of every kind. All industry is controlled by the central government. In fact, every aspect of the economy in set in motion from the top. What I reported was learned by talking to Berliners on the ship and on land. And from the government controlled news media and radio broadcasts.

"There is a new spirit abroad in Germany and it goes something like this: The war was lost for stupid reasons, the victory belonged to Germans; the Treaties were unfair and punitive. All German speaking peoples should be united under one flag; the fatherland will rise and the future belongs to Germany." Willie stopped for breath. He hadn't put this much effort into his report.

"Everything economic, political or cultural is controlled by the Nazi party under the leadership of a prophet, Adolph Hitler who speaks with the power of hate and revenge. I fear for the country and its people." Willie looked at Herman for a sign that he understood.

All that Herman had experienced in the military he considered good. He had not seen prejudice against Jews, they were in the army and unsegregated. His partner had been Jewish. The Night of Broken Glass was news to Herman. His memories were clouded only by the unwillingness of his German family and the military to let him return to America when his training ended. He decided then that it must be because of his skills but it was a painful experience to recall. He thought twice about what Willie was saying.

Herman finally spoke. "If there is war, will we be suspect as happened during the last war?"

Willie looked grim. "I hope not. Watch your back and your mouth, Herman. No pro-German defenses in public now. And I plan to make contact with people at West Point to be sure Frederick will not have a problem. I am only an in-law. Frederick is Frank's son."

Eva Emilia had joined them just in time to hear her Uncle's last words. She was stunned. The whole idea of the visit to Germany seemed wrong to her. Economically speaking, it was not right to schedule an ocean voyage to see a brother-in-law who stayed resolutely out of touch. She now learned of the assignment and her father's work. Unlike Herman and Frederick, it did not concern her. Her journey towards a full medical degree in obstetrics and gynecology was almost completed. Eva had nothing but praise from medical staff and from patients. There were inequities she would work on over time, perhaps with help from Elise and Louisa, but her next years would fulfill all of her dreams. She was not Frederick's little sister now, she was, almost, Eva Freimarck, MD.

After Eva left, the brothers thought of the rest of the family and the need to alert the others. They decided to tell Max only that his father was well and working in Germany. Charles was in Hollywood. With Brigitte. It didn't appear that Frank's choice of work would affect them in any way they could foresee. This eliminated two more possible confidants. They resolved to contact each other if any further names came to mind. As of now, they were finished. Louisa would hear only the surface news, not the dark underside. They shook hands, as brothers do after a certain age. Long ago they would have pricked their thumbs and exchanged a drop of blood.

The next day Herman reported back to work at the Dayton base. They had been told of his talk and were delighted by the good publicity. Willie returned to the classroom and left with a box of term papers he had forgotten he assigned in his absence. All seemed well and Elise mentioned none of this at the firm. Louisa was equally silent in her school. The hope of all was that Frank would continue to ignore them.

Chapter 37

The Law of the Land

Elise told Max that his father was safe and working in Germany for a short time longer. Max had not enjoyed a close relationship with his father and so the news was not painful. He listened as patiently as possible and then asked Elise if she could recommend a current case for him to study for his thesis.

Several issues came to mind. The rights of labor were high on her priority list as she saw the suffering in the German community and in the family business. Workers' celebrated recent Supreme Court decisions affirming labor unions, free speech, and free press. The question would be whether the law was followed or challenged when it was not. Religious freedom was addressed through the Jehovah's Witnesses' rights, process rights in criminal cases were defended as were the rights of currently unpopular groups. This would be Elise's choice. All of these efforts were showing slow progress in the nation as a whole.

Intolerance of radical political beliefs permitted the execution of some and the murder of others who deviated from the norm. Fear of anarchy led to the acceptance of dictatorial powers in countries abroad. This must be watched in America.

Some bumps slowed full steam ahead and some did not. Texas proposed a white only access rule during primary voting controlled by the State legislature. It was decided by the Supreme Court that political parties enjoyed voluntary membership and they could discriminate. School segregation and separate but equal still held sway in some places but the practice was slowly dying. Thurgood Marshall challenged this and won entry of a black student to the University of Maryland School of Law. But an anti-lynching law did not pass and Jim Crow laws remained strong in the south.

In all, the decade delivered hope for the future. It provided a base of issues and concerns that would need to be revisited over the coming years.

Elise had neatly summarized the thinking of those lawyers she knew. The Supreme Court cases were on the tip of her tongue. Looking at Max, Elise decided he should find out more on his own, not at his mother's knee. She was fairly certain she knew the direction he would take. He did not disappoint her.

"As you know, mother, I have been attending meetings of the NAACP with Letitia. Their list is long and I believe I will assess their identified needs before choosing. One area is of great interest to me as an American: how much autonomy should States have over issues that conflict with the Constitution? And I should add, the recent Constitutional Amendments." Max stopped to write this down. He had a specific question in mind but thought it best to keep it private.

Ohio, like many States, had prohibited marriage between white and black citizens, or if not marriage, they were banned from living together as man and wife. Usually, it was called a felony, punishable by fine or imprisonment. That law was rescinded but in practice, miscegenation remained an issue. Max felt the 14th amendment clearly addressed this issue and any laws denying equality were unconstitutional.

"Just your opinion, mother. Do you feel I should avoid an issue that is black and white to me but completely controversial to others? Perhaps even in a law firm?"

Elise answered without a second thought. "Max, if good people hesitate to challenge what is wrong, progress will stop entirely. Your question is one many ask themselves often and some choose to take the easy way by conforming. You could argue that once a lawyer you would have more power to address what is wrong. The hesitation I hear is the real Max. Do what you feel you must, but let it be a decision you can live with all of your life."

"You have been a great help. I will let you know my choice as soon as I've made it." Max kissed Elise on her now wrinkled cheek, smiled, and left the room. He had made his decision.

Elise looked around the bedroom that was the heart of the house for her. Over the years she had watched the andirons blacken and drapes become shabby. Only her closest family and friends would see this evidence of time passing. The Rookwood fireplace still dominated the room. The chairs that faced it had been occupied through the years by a young couple, two friends, her mother, and now by Max and herself. In every instance she felt a compulsion to search for the truth and she was never sorry.

Max's problem was partly academic. There was the constitution and the 14th Amendment. There were national laws and State laws, some relevant and some not. And then, there were the practices that defied the laws. He was well aware of issues surrounding the rights of all citizens to vote. He was distressed by the ease of segregating neighborhoods through local zoning laws, in part to influence voting outcomes. And the schools, especially the private schools and universities, were not fully transparent when selecting new students. Even when accepted, black students were often in separate (but equal?) classrooms. These were issues he could write about with passion, logic, and facts.

The other issues were the numerous responses to interracial marriage across the country. This was personal. Max loved Letitia. He had not told her or demonstrated his love, not because of cowardice but because he feared a life together might be a constant struggle. Their children would be born with a burden they did not deserve. He had no idea of Letitia's feelings. They had both been careful to avoid any emotion outside of friendship. He would sleep on it. Tomorrow was right around the corner.

The black population was growing as jobs appeared in local industries. He wanted to know the policies of the Cincinnati public schools. This would serve as a benchmark. The city was on the border of north and south. What made the biggest impact on education? What was the core of education? And who were the educators?

The next day, Max was waiting outside Louisa's school. He wanted to talk to her while the day was still fresh in her mind and no family problems pushed the classroom into second place. He stopped her at the end of the school steps and they drove away together.

Louisa looked tired but happy. Her classroom was her inspiration. She was especially interested in bringing the poorer students to their full potential and many of them did reach the same level of learning as their more affluent classmates. "Max, I think I know why you are here but it would be less stressful if you tell me why and what you hope to accomplish."

"I am on a mission, Louisa. My bar exam is next month and if I am not in a profession where I can follow my beliefs, I will not even try to pass it. I mean to continue working towards erasing the 'separate' part of the current dictates. I am looking to equality: black and white, Asian, Jehovah's Witness, transgender, or even women. All must be equal under the law." Max was surprised at his speech. He hadn't been sure of his goal when he started.

He continued, "What do you see happening in your school, are the children treated as equals?

Louisa did not hold back. She was Elise's friend and she cared for Max. With no desire to hurt either, she answered Max as she believed. "It is not equal. If not in elementary school, it is not after that. Each student does not have opportunity, support, and encouragement. Or even food. They are prepared to enter adulthood without seeking even the same chance to choose their home's location or the University they want to attend. It must change. And Max, please consider the black woman. Her place is many times the hardest."

Whenever the question of Civil Rights arose, one concern led to another. There was no part of society unaffected by race, religion, or gender. The slow ending of the depression gave hope for a better society. Max saw his place as the identifier of wrongs to be righted. This was surely the time when this could happen: the future belonged to those who sought justice.

Later Max realized what was really pushing his decision. He had been so concentrated on his own problem he had not followed the course of events. Elise had told him that Gertrud's grandchildren had been called "Huns".

"They are still in short pants! They are American all the way! What is happening to the world of progress and peace?"

Chapter 38

The World is Melting

"The whole world is melting!" Elise was speaking much louder than usual. "In some places it is melting into a solid mass with all extraneous pieces thrown away. Only one race remains to be celebrated as supreme. In others, the melt produces a variety of contents, all equal in worth. For example, in America, the Founding Fathers wrote a document that proclaimed equality and our laws reflect that."

Louise spoke in a whisper with the intent of being overheard. "A few founding mothers might have been helpful."

The laughter broke some of the solemnity of the group. Louisa had a knack of deflating the pompous and making her point with levity. "True enough," Augusta laughed and considered the metaphor. And what happens now?"

"Make no mistake. America will fight at some point. Ours is not a country to suffer fools and tyrants. I am worried for Frederick and all young men who will be called. This is principle and it amazes me that we have been neutral so long." Gertrud thought of grandchildren who were on the verge of adulthood and who would be swept away in war as happens when there is a challenge.

The women had met to discuss the recent suspicion leveled at German-Americans. Once again, their patriotism was questioned, if not personally, as a group. The globe seemed on fire and the people were frightened, angry, and looking for the enemy everywhere. Although Augusta and Gertrud were insulated by their husbands' origins, those named Freimarck carried a recognizable label.

Immigration quotas were specific and the number of immigrants declined each year. Restrictions on immigrants multiplied. Those so=called hyphenated Americans were fewer and many of those in the country had little connection or memory of their roots. Unless your ancestry reached back to the Mayflower, being foreign born was not a good item for a resume.

It appeared that the majority of America's citizens still wanted neutrality. The President followed their dictate, at least publically. Lend lease was working and ships, planes, and munitions were sent across the Atlantic after Congress lifted the embargo. As one European country after another fell to the German military, the more difficult it was to hold back total commitment to the fast escalating war.

The move towards autocratic governments could be noted in Germany, Italy, Russia, Yugoslavia, Greece, Spain and Poland. Each was different but the result of this move away from democratic government in any form was there for all to see. None had the military might of Germany.

Jean Romano

The devastation in Europe and on the sea brought more Americans into the movement towards war. There was something to fight for and something to fight against. A few young men had joined in the battle in Spain before war seemed inevitable. More were inspired now. And yet the divisions in America were still present. They were not on party lines but on the familiar issue of race.

Throughout the nation's history the question of black soldiers led to debate and various solutions. For many, the idea of arming blacks was impossible although many had served in the American fighting forces since Revolutionary War times. Sadly, Jim Crow laws and mentality carried on into World War II.

Divisions were segregated. Blacks were limited to support roles, for example, cooks or gravediggers. The Air Force created the Tuskegee Air Men as a segregated branch and they became celebrated aviators.

Black nurses were denied admission at first. When accepted, they were assigned to black servicemen's wards. The number accepted had a quota. This policy ended in 1941 when their value and the need for nurses overcame whatever scruples the medical corps held.

As the '30's moved on, more nations turned to isolation, nationalism, and autocracy in some form. Italy ran the trains on time under a fascist leader, and Germany's National Socialists were defying the caveats of the post-war treaties. Under it all was the specter of race and religion.

The "great race" the Aryans or Nordic peoples were elevated in Germany under the leadership of the country's Fuehrer. Jews were denied all public offices and forced out of Universities whether professors or students. Dissidents were purged from government office. Gypsies, homosexuals, and the disabled were scheduled for extermination.

The list was long. Labor Unions disappeared, education was monitored, and the press and speech were no longer free of Nazi propaganda. White supremacy was called forth with pride. As was the Fuehrer.

Lists are easy to create. Hitler's Youth program instituted physical fitness and expected full loyalty. Young boys sang *and the future belongs to me* in praise of the fatherland. The next years prepared for this to happen. Industrialists pledged loyalty and armaments and technology were rapidly transforming German industries. Manpower was allocated to industry through the central government and the capital in German banks was also under government control. Women were exhorted to follow the old mantra of "kirche, kinder, and kuchen." The population needed to grow and that was the women's job.

Pages from the black codes of Jim Crow in the American south supplied the Nazi party with models of repression. The Great Race would be pure enough to lead the entire world. And the German army was on the move.

~~~

In America, prosperity was returning. The New Deal promulgated by Franklin Delano Roosevelt guaranteed the bank deposits of small investors. The Security Exchange Commission monitored the sale of stocks and equities. A series of public works projects began and the Tennessee Valley Authority brought power to an area long in need of federal assistance. Social Security was in place for the disabled and elderly. The National Labor Relations Board was created to give workers redress in a time of giant corporations.

White flight continued to change cities. Whole areas became black, Appalachian, Asian or populated by minority groups. Over the Rhine in Cincinnati remained as before the war.

The American people would not to be caught up in another European war. Or any war. Families were protective of their young men and did not want to see a repeat of the losses of World War I.

And yet the world wobbled into another war, country by country, family by family. The third generation of immigrants from Germany would be involved as the Holtz and Freimarck men and women found roles to play in America. Differences were put aside and a united front answered the call.

Chapter 39

The Families Survives and Thrives

'The Holtz and Freimarck families were widely dispersed. Names changed but there would always be someone named Frank and someone named William. They were one picture of American diversity. Many served in the armed forces and the army air corps was as much an attraction as NASA would be to Herman's grandchildren.

Herman's twin boys, born late in his life, produced many grandchildren to carry on the Holtz name. Angelika was delighted to spend her days in the kitchen with her children, but not in church. As decided when they married, the boys were brought up in the Jewish faith. Greta cried when she heard of the birth, but she sobbed with happiness when her sister told her of Herman's acceptance of their religion.

Willie had a firm hold on Keynsian economics favored by the President. He often wrote papers explaining how high tariffs affected production and consumption but self-sufficiency ruled the day in planning despite his careful explanations. His main concern, after preparing and delivering lectures in the classroom, was how to assist allies prepare and defeat the German army. His own passion was to protect them in the fight for democracy.

Louisa listened to his lectures on policy but her own effort was to protect the interests of women and children in the workplace. Her classroom received all her energy. Willie and Louisa had no children but influenced their nieces and nephews and saw the University of Cincinnati embrace many of them.

It was heard from refugees that the purge of Jews from Nazi Germany, most recently of those in government positions, continued throughout the period before and during the Second World War. The label of Jewish went back for generations and the family were concerned about Franks' ancestry. They dismissed this as foolish but Frank was never located after peace returned. His brother, Willie, and son, Max, did make a trip to Germany but no records of Frank Freimarck were found.

Charles found a job promoting patriotism through films. He never became an actor but he did produce an unending stream of patriotic bits that were used in movie theaters. Eventually he became the editor of news releases and was acknowledged for his ability to encapsulate events in a short clip.

Brigitte found her place in commercial films as an extra. She married a young man from New York and they returned to his hometown after the war. Augusta was proud of her son and thankful that he did not live near her. His explanation of why he did not marry gave her good reason to encourage his life in Hollywood. He doesn't have a star on the magic walk of Hollywood fame but he is remembered for his ability to produce images that stayed in people's minds and hearts.

Eva Emilia was an excellent doctor who expanded her practice as new medicines and treatments were discovered. She became active in Planned Parenthood and was known to help those who needed a steady and non-judgmental diagnosis. Few women died in childbirth under her care. Her husband, also a doctor, became a leader in prosthetics and helped Willie walk through his golden years. Their son, Frank, was named in honor of the father Eva E. had for a short while.

Max and Letitia married later in life than they planned. They thought seriously about choices and decided to leave Cincinnati, depriving Elise of one grandchild but visiting often.

Gertrud's daughters were different from one another and from almost anyone else. Except for her oldest that was a very contented housewife, Elizabeth and Jane moved in the highest circles of Washington, but not in society. They championed the role of women in war at the Department of Labor.

And Elise, the Lorelei of the Rhine, although transplanted to The Ohio, finished her days with satisfaction. She had never shirked an issue she uncovered. Eva Emilia could be followed closely, and Max lived a purposeful life with the support of his mother and his lifelong love, Letitia. When Elise died, family leadership passed to Louisa and Augusta who bonded long ago in the fight for Women's Suffrage.

Epilogue

100 Years Later

"I can't find one damn thing I'm looking for! Where's my radio?" Old Max was on another of his tirades. 'Who is there? I can hear you! Why isn't there anyone here that I know?"

"They're dead." Young Frank, who wasn't so young anymore, responded.

"Well then, youngster, suppose you step up to the plate." Max was feeling more like himself today. Usually he just looked around and decided life was not worth living. "I would like to speak to the manager of this place. Or to my great grandson Frederick."

Young Frank's wife looked in without revealing her presence. "Where is Assisted Living when you need it." She sounded as hopeless as her husband. "I thought you were going to tell him that Frederick was out in space."

"Tried that but he knew he landed years ago."

"How could he know that? He doesn't know anything that I mention." Clara didn't just sound hopeless. She was. Max had been living with them for the past three years but it seemed more like thirty. Assisted Living had been dismantled by the State. Unless you were actively dying, Independence at Home was the fall back. Of course, it was assumed that it would be with help. Caregiving was a college major now. Government sponsored In Home Care was guaranteed.

"Has he had his meds yet, Mr. Frank?" The Tuesday morning caregiver moved into the room with the ease of a resident. He was.

Frank muttered under his breath and turning his head to face Great Grandpa Max, he spoke softly to the aide. "He has been medicated two or three times but nothing changes. Why bother? And don't try saying anything else in English, I know it is a stretch."

Pablo stopped, looked at Frank, and said, "Coño." He added for fun, "Tomorrow is payday."

The country had moved on since Max was a kid. All were now entitled to spend their last years aging in place with help paid for by Medicaid. If you didn't qualify by reason of capital gains, your last living kin were billed and enlisted for your care.

Max entered the conversation. In a low voice he asked Frank, "Is Pablo black?"

Frank answered just as quietly. "No, he is brown. I am black."

"Good." Will was satisfied that all was well.

Sources

Books:

Axelrod, Alan. (1999). The Complete Idiot's Guide to 20th Century History. Alpha Books.

Beard, Charles A. (1957). The Economic Basis of Politics. New York: Vintage Book.

Beard, Charles A. Mary R. Beard. (1960). New Basic History of the United States. Garden City N.Y. :Doubleday & Co.

Ergang, Robert. (1953). Europe In Our Time. D.C. Heath & Co.

Hancock, M. Donald and Henry Krisch. (2009). Washington, D.C. CQ Press.

Hynowitz, Carol, Michaele Weisman. (1998). New York: Bantam Books.

Manchester, William. (1963). The Arms of Krupp. Boston: Little, Brown & Co.

Samuelson, Paul. ((1951). Economics: An Introductory Analysis. New York: McGraw-Hill Book Company Inc.

Wallbank, Walter T., Alastair Taylor. (1949). Civilization: Past and Present. Scott, New York: Foresman & Company.

Web Sites: General Information

ACLU History (aclu.org)

Staff of the Ohio History Connection. "Cincinnati, Ohio". (info@ohiohistory.org)

Guide to African-American Resources. Cincinnati History Library and Archives

League of Women Voters Through the Decades Wikipedia (LWV,org)

University of Cincinnati History (info@ohiohistory.org)

West Point in 1930's (westpoint.edu)

Articles:

Frazier, Ian. Old Hatreds. (August 26, 2019). The New Yorker.

Leonhart, David. Op Ed. (September 6, 2019).New York Times.

Little, Becky. (May 11, 2018). When German Immigrants Were America's Undesirables. History Stories.

Silverstein, Barrett A. (Spring, 2004). 1920's A Decade of Change. The Heel Junior Historian Association. NC Museum of History.

Waxman, Olivia B. (July 19, 2019). 'It Just Goes On and On': How the Race Riots of 1919's 'Red Summer' Helpd Shape a Century of American History. Time.com. History Newsletter.

Printed in the United States
By Bookmasters